Not Until This Moment

-A Hope Springs Novella-

Valerie M. Bodden

Not Until This Moment © 2019 by Valerie M. Bodden.

This is a work of fiction. Names, characters, places and incidents either are products of the author's imagination or used in a fictitious manner. Any resemblance to any person, living or dead, is coincidental.

Cover design: Ideal Book Covers

Valerie M. Bodden

Visit me at www.valeriembodden.com

Hope Springs Series

Not Until Christmas

Not Until Forever

Not Until This Moment

Not Until You

Not Until Us

Not Until Christmas Morning

Not Until This Day

Not Until Someday

Not Until Now

Not Until Then

Not Until The End

River Falls Series

Pieces of Forever

Songs of Home

Memories of the Heart

Whispers of Truth

Contents

A Gift for You...

Members of my Reader's Club get a FREE book, available exclusively to my subscribers. When you sign up, you'll also be the first to know about new releases, book deals, and giveaways.

Simply visit www.valeriembodden.com/gift to join!

"For I know the plans I have for you," *declares the Lord, "plans to prosper you and not to harm you, plans to give you hope and a future."*

JEREMIAH 29:11

Chapter 1

*P*eyton wiped her frosting-smudged hands on her apron and eased the kitchen door open to peek into the empty ballroom. Her eyes roamed the elegant table settings, the tall vases filled with amaryllis and orchids, the fairy lights that floated above the room like stars. The bride and groom were at the church, probably exchanging their vows at this very moment, but soon they'd come into this perfect room. Peyton could picture exactly how the bride's face would look. She'd seen that look on every bride's face at every wedding she'd ever been to. It was the look that said this was the happiest day of her life.

Peyton pulled her head back and let the door close, barely suppressing a sigh.

A year ago, she'd thought her own happily ever after was just around the corner. But now it seemed further away than ever.

Leah bustled past with a stack of serving bowls. She shuffled them and reached over to pat Peyton's arm, the same way she had at every wedding they'd worked together in the past year.

Peyton straightened her shoulders and marched to the counter. Standing here dwelling on regrets wouldn't get the cake done.

She surveyed the four tiers she'd already stacked and grabbed her bench scraper to smooth the spots where her fingers had left impressions in the buttercream, exposing the red velvet swirl underneath. It was exactly what she would have picked for her own wedding cake—if Jared had ever proposed.

She blinked against the sting behind her eyelids. She had to stop feeling this way every time she set up a wedding cake. It'd been almost a year since he'd told her he never intended to get married. Almost a year since she'd decided she couldn't be with a man who couldn't commit to a future with her. Almost a year since she'd pulverized her own heart when she'd broken up with him.

Time to move on.

With a sudden decisiveness, she grabbed her piping materials and filled them with the buttercream she was

8

becoming famous for. Okay, maybe not famous, but well-known enough around Hope Springs to keep her busy most weekends of the summer and even a few in winter—like this one. She set to work adding the delicate beading the couple had requested for the edges of their cake. She let the noises around her fade as she concentrated on making each tiny circle perfect, just barely connecting it to the next one. The intense focus was soothing.

"You're coming to Tamarack with us next weekend, right?" Leah's voice right next to her made Peyton jump, and she almost yanked the piping tip back from the cake. Fortunately, years of practice had given her a steady hand, even in the face of Leah's enthusiasm. She finished the last four beads, then pulled the tip away and spun the cake to examine her work. Not too bad.

"It's perfect." Leah pretended to swipe a finger toward the frosting, but Peyton batted her hand away.

"Tell me you're coming, or I'll do it." Leah held a finger toward the cake again, her eyebrows waggling as if daring Peyton to tempt her.

Too bad Peyton knew it was an empty threat. Leah didn't have an unkind bone in her body, and she'd never ruin Peyton's work—or a couple's wedding cake.

"I don't think so." Peyton couldn't meet Leah's eyes. She hated to disappoint anyone, least of all the friend who'd come to feel like a sister, but there was no way she could go on the annual skiing trip. Not if Jared was going to be there. And anyway, he was the only reason she'd been invited in the first place. Now that they weren't together, it would be awkward if she tagged along.

"Sawyer specifically told me to make sure you knew you were still invited." Drat Leah's ability to read her mind.

"I'm sure he was only being polite."

Unlike the others who went on the trip every year, Peyton hadn't grown up in Hope Springs. She'd only met Sawyer a few years ago when she'd gone with Jared and his friends to the ski resort Sawyer's family owned.

"Well, if he was, then saying no would be rude." Leah gave her an impish smile, obviously certain she'd won the argument.

But Peyton was tougher than that. "I have another wedding that weekend." Which also happened to be Valentine's Day. Not that she cared about her former favorite holiday anymore.

"I know. I'm catering that one, too. But we'll be back by Wednesday. Try again."

Peyton reviewed her mental calendar. Why couldn't she come up with something else?

"So it's really about Jared." Leah gave her the same half-sympathetic, half-stern look she did every time Jared's name came up.

Peyton snatched her scraper and smoothed a nonexistent dent. Of course it was about Jared. "Don't you have a wedding dinner to get ready?"

Leah planted a hand on her hip. "You said you were over Jared."

She had said that. Multiple times. She'd told it to herself every day, hoping that one of these days it would be true.

"I am over him. I just—"

"Then prove it." Leah crossed her arms in front of her. "If you're over him, you won't have a problem coming skiing with all of us. Maybe you'll meet someone new."

Peyton studied her friend. She should say no. Leah was intentionally pushing her buttons. But her friend knew her well. Knew she was incapable of backing down from a challenge.

"Fine," she huffed. "I'll come. Now let me finish this cake."

Leah gave her a triumphant smile and a quick squeeze. "Gotta run. I have a wedding dinner to prepare." She rushed to the other side of the kitchen, where the rest of her crew worked to unload carts filled with chicken, potatoes, and all kinds of food that made Peyton's mouth water.

Peyton shook her head and tried to force her concentration back to her work. This was one challenge she should have walked away from.

Chapter 2

*J*ared drove the monstrous conversion van he'd just picked up into the parking lot of the Hidden Cafe.

He'd been waiting for this Friday morning for weeks now. He was ready for this ski trip like he'd been ready for few things in his life. The past year had been rough, and he needed to get out of Hope Springs for a few days. Just enough time to clear his head. To escape the constant fear of running into Peyton. To finally get over her.

As if that will ever happen.

But it had to happen. Peyton had made it clear what she wanted—marriage, a life together, a family. Much as he would do anything to give her the moon and stars, the thing she was asking for—that was the one thing he couldn't give her.

Which didn't stop him from glancing around the parking lot, just in case her car was here.

That sinking feeling in his stomach when he didn't spot it was stupid. He'd known she wouldn't come this year. Or any year, now that they weren't together.

He turned off the vehicle and jumped out. Anyway, it was for the best, he reminded himself as he strode into the Hidden Cafe.

The moment he stepped through the door, he stopped to inhale deeply, just as he did whenever he came here. The scents of home cooking got him every time. His home had never smelled like this growing up.

It had smelled more like . . .

Did fear have a smell?

"Hey, man." Ethan clapped a hand on his shoulder. "Got some muffins for the road." He opened the paper bag in his hand and pulled out a giant muffin, passing it to Jared.

"Thanks." Jared took a big bite of the still-warm pastry, savoring the apple and cinnamon melting on his tongue. "Everyone here?"

"Just about. Ariana's over there." Ethan glowed at the mere mention of his wife's name. "And Leah. Her brother Dan is coming, too. I guess he just moved back to town to serve with his dad at the church."

Jared nodded shortly. He didn't need to know what was going on at the church.

"Emma's on her way. And Sophie and Spencer just called. They'll be here in a few minutes, and they're bringing Spencer's brother Tyler. Vi can't make it this year. She didn't want to close the store."

Jared tallied the group in his head. "So we've got five here, and we're waiting for four."

"Actually—" Ethan cleared his throat and didn't meet Jared's eyes. "We're waiting for five."

Jared did a quick recount. "I only count four."

"That's because you're not counting Peyton."

"Pey—" Jared ran a hand up and down his rough cheek. "Peyton's coming?" His throat went dry. He'd been so sure she wouldn't come. So sure he'd be able to use this time to get over her.

Ethan watched him. "You okay with that?"

Jared gave a tight smile and a quick nod. "Of course."

But Ethan tipped his head to the side. His partner on the volunteer first responder squad knew him better than anyone else. Knew how hard not being with Peyton had been for him. He was the only one who knew why Jared would never marry, too.

"Well, I guess I'm going to have to be, aren't I?" he muttered as the door opened and Peyton stepped inside.

Jared caught his breath as her eyes landed on his for a second, then skipped away. Her mouth was set into a faint scowl as she gazed past him, clearly searching for someone else—probably anyone else.

He shuffled to the side to get out of her way. No reason to make this harder than it had to be.

Her lips curled into a smile, and for half a heartbeat he let himself think it was for him. But she slid past him and let Leah wrap her into a hug.

Jared tried not to think about how long it had been since his arms had been around Peyton. Tried not to notice how they ached to hold her again.

So far so good on being okay with this.

He moved toward the door. "We should get the van loaded." He said it loudly so everyone would hear, but his gaze locked on Peyton and refused to budge. She wore the white ski jacket with pink trim he had helped her pick out the first year they'd gone skiing together. Her pale hair was swept into some kind of messy bun on top of her head, making her look casual and sophisticated at the same time. And her eyes. Her eyes were what had drawn him to her in the first place. So impossibly light they were almost transparent. But it was more than their color. It was their warmth. Their sincerity. The way they revealed everything she felt.

Which was also what scared him about them.

He held the door as Ethan and Ariana filed past, then waited for the others.

But Leah was introducing Peyton to a dark-haired guy with his back to Jared.

When Peyton smiled at the guy and held out a hand to shake his, Jared's stomach clenched. He'd been waiting for the moment he learned she'd met someone else. But that didn't mean he wanted to witness it.

His eyes flicked to hers again. But all he saw in them was polite interest as she talked to the stranger.

After a second, the three of them moved toward the door. Caught watching them, Jared considered making an escape out to the van. But he couldn't very well close the door in their faces.

He stood his ground as they approached.

Peyton passed through first, barely acknowledging him, though he was pretty sure he heard a mumbled "thanks" before she scooted toward the van. That woman couldn't bear to be impolite, even to him.

"Hey, Jared." He tore his eyes off Peyton's retreating figure and forced them to Leah. "You remember my little brother Dan? He was a couple years behind us in school."

Little brother? The guy easily stood two inches taller than Jared's six feet.

The guy gave Jared a warm smile and held out a hand. "Thanks for letting me tag along."

Jared returned the handshake. "No problem." *As long as you don't steal my girlfriend.*

But that wasn't right. If Dan ended up with Peyton, he wouldn't be stealing her. Jared had already let her go.

Too bad his heart didn't know that yet.

Outside, Sophie, Spencer, Tyler, and Emma were getting out of their cars. Jared opened the back of the van and everyone stashed their bags, exchanging greetings and laughs as they did. Only Peyton seemed quiet.

The moment he opened the doors of the van, she launched herself inside and scooted to the corner of the backseat.

Clearly, she wasn't going to be riding shotgun this year.

Jared waited for the others to load into the vehicle, then jumped in, glancing at Leah, who'd taken the seat next to him.

"We ready for this?" Jared turned the ignition as a resounding chorus of yeses hit his ears.

As he backed out of the spot, his eyes flicked to the rearview mirror. They landed instantly on Peyton, but she was staring out the window, her lips drawn into a thin line.

He was tempted to tell a stupid joke, the way he had a hundred times before to erase that look from her face. But this time he was pretty sure hearing from him would only make the line thinner.

Chapter 3

*T*rees. Trees. And more trees.

The view never changed.

Not that Peyton didn't like trees. Especially when they glinted with a dusting of snow as these did.

But it was taking a monumental effort to keep her gaze directed out the window. If she let herself peek into the car for even one second, her eyes would seek out Jared. And that electric current she'd felt during the brief second their gazes had collided in the cafe this morning had been enough to warn her away.

She'd never get over him if she couldn't look at him without feeling their connection. So she just wouldn't look at him.

"We're here." Jared's voice reached to the back of the van, a hint of weariness behind the words, and she couldn't help it.

Her eyes tracked to the rearview mirror, and she caught a glimpse of the short stubble on his cheeks and the sharp line of his nose. The color-changing hazel of his eyes. Fortunately, he was peering ahead, not into the mirror.

She shifted her gaze away before he could catch her looking.

Jared steered the van down the long, winding driveway that led to the ski lodge. Peyton focused out the window again, peering toward the massive building. It was chic in a retro-mid-century-modern sort of way, everything chunky and angular and oversized. The first time she'd come here, she'd found it garish, but it'd grown on her. Now she could see how it worked against the backdrop of rolling snow-covered hills and the sharp lines of the trees.

They passed a small stable, with several horses grazing in a paddock beyond it, and Peyton's heart jumped. She could still pick out the two she and Jared had ridden last time they were here. Was that really only a year ago? How had everything gone so wrong since then?

That weekend, she'd been so sure Jared would ask her to marry him. She'd even thought it might be while they were out riding horses. What could be more romantic?

Horses. Snowfall. Privacy. It was like God had set everything up for the perfect proposal.

Except it had never come.

Peyton had tried not to be disappointed. Tried to tell herself it didn't mean anything. That Jared was probably waiting for the next weekend—for Valentine's Day, when they'd be back home in Hope Springs. After all, they'd been together three years already, and she knew without a doubt that he loved her. She just wanted to make it official and start their life together.

She had waited until the last possible moment on Valentine's Day, after they'd gone out to dinner, after they'd strolled along the lakefront, after they'd done everything romantic she could think of. But when he'd walked her to her door and said goodnight, when he'd turned and walked down her porch steps, when he'd almost reached his car, she couldn't hold it back any longer.

It had started to rain, a cold, miserable February rain, but she didn't care that she was getting wet. She needed to know.

"Jared." She didn't recognize the way his name came out of her mouth.

He turned so, so slowly, and she could read it in the tension in his shoulders. He knew what she was going to ask. Knew what she wanted. And his answer wasn't going to be what she wanted to hear. But she had to ask anyway.

"Do you think we'll ever get married?"

His mouth opened, but no words came out. He just stood there, blinking at her. Finally, he closed the space between them. Grabbed her hands. Pulled her to him so that her head rested on his chest.

"Peyton, I love you more than anything in this world."

The words should have melted her, should have reassured her, but they didn't. She knew there was a "but" behind them.

"But—"

She tensed, but he didn't let her go. "But I don't plan to ever get married. That's not something—" He swallowed. "That's not something I can do."

"But—" She had to fight for breath. "But why not? If you love me?" She felt like her heart had morphed into an ice sculpture and he was chipping away at it with an ice pick.

He gripped her shoulders, slid her back a little, and waited until she lifted her face toward his. "I *do* love you.

No matter what else, you have to know that. But I— I just can't."

"I don't understand. Why can't you?" She was so desperate to understand. To help him see he was wrong, that he could marry. That they *should* marry.

But he simply shook his head and turned around, dragging himself back to his car. "I'm sorry."

"You're sorry?" She was stunned, speechless. She had been so sure he was the one.

As a kid, her mom had told her so many times how she'd known Peyton's dad was the one. He'd made her laugh. He'd made her feel safe and secure and treasured. He'd encouraged her in her faith. And Peyton had felt all those things with Jared. She'd prayed for him as if he were her future husband. So how could he not be the one?

Jared's shoulders slumped as he opened his car door.

"Wait, Jared." Peyton wanted to run to him, to tell him it was okay if he didn't want to marry yet. That they could wait. That if he never decided to marry, she'd be okay with it.

But she knew none of that was true. She wanted a husband, a family. A future.

And if he couldn't be the one to give her that, she had to let him go.

"If you don't—" She stopped to choke down the sob working its way up from her core. "If you don't love me enough to commit to me before God and our friends and family, to want to make a life with me, then you don't love me the way I need to be loved." She gulped at the air to force the next words out. "I don't think we should see each other anymore."

Jared had dropped his head onto the top of his car then, wrapping his arms over it like he was sheltering from a blow. She'd longed to go to him. But she'd kept her feet planted, letting the tears drop down her cheeks faster than the rain. When he'd lifted his head, his face had glistened with moisture. But he'd nodded once, then he'd slid into his car and driven away.

And the ice sculpture that had become her heart had fractured into a million pieces that could never be repaired.

"Going to sit in here all day?"

Peyton's head jerked up at the voice, pulling her out of her memories.

Jared stood at the side door of the van, lips twisted into the tiniest smile. The other seats in the vehicle were all empty, and voices drifted from outside as the others gathered their stuff.

"Yeah." She straightened her stiff legs and hunched over to climb past the empty seats. Jared held out a hand to help her, but she ignored it. If looking at him wasn't safe, touching him would be catastrophic.

Once out of the van, she dashed to the back to grab her threadbare old duffel bag, which was packed so full she'd barely been able to zip it.

It was heavier than she remembered, and she sized up the long walk across the parking lot to the lodge entrance. Jared usually carried her bags for her—teasing her about how many books she packed—but this year she was on her own. Out of the corner of her eye, she noticed Jared watching her, and she could almost see his internal debate about whether to take her bag for her.

Well, she'd make that decision for him. She hefted the bag in front of her and wrapped both arms around it.

By the time they made it to the building, her shoulders and back screamed with the strain, but she kept a smile pasted on her face as Jared held the door for them all. The moment they reached the check-in desk, she dropped the bag to the floor with a relieved sigh.

She stretched her arms over her head and gazed around the lobby as Ethan checked the group in. A fire roared in the huge stone fireplace that rose from a sunken area in the middle of the lobby all the way to the top of the building two stories above. A few people lounged on the built-in couches that surrounded it. That's where she planned to hide out most of the trip. Away from the ski hills where Jared would spend his days.

Sawyer popped out from his office in the back to greet them all. When he got to Peyton, he leaned in to give her a quick hug and whispered, "I'm glad you came. Jared is an idiot to have let you go."

"Thanks." Peyton pulled away with a smile she hoped didn't look as awkward as it felt.

A second later, she was again staggering under the weight of her bag as they made their way across the lobby. They always skipped the lodge's slow, clunky elevator in favor of the stairs. Somehow, she got wedged in between Jared and the wall as they began to climb. The subtle, spicy-sweet bergamot cologne she'd have recognized in her sleep washed over her. How could the scent alone be enough to conjure up the feel of his arms around her? She smooshed herself closer to the wall.

Leah handed out keys as they walked. Leah, Emma, Sophie, and Peyton would share one room. Tyler, Spencer, Jared, and Dan would have another, and Ethan and Ariana would have their own. Peyton pushed down a stab of jealousy. Since the first time she'd come here with Jared, she'd looked forward to the day when they could share a room as husband and wife.

"Oh, no." Leah counted the remaining keys in her hand. "We're one key short for the girls' room."

"I'll go grab one." Peyton whirled around before anyone else could offer. She couldn't handle walking next to Jared a second longer. Even if it meant climbing back down and then up the stairs with her ridiculously heavy bag.

"At least let me take your bag for you." Jared's voice was low enough that she doubted any of the others heard.

"I've got it." She ignored the way the muscles in her shoulders knotted as she barreled down the steps and practically ran across the lobby to the check-in desk.

Sawyer was talking to the young clerk there, but he broke off with a huge smile the moment she reached them.

"Peyton. I'm glad you came back down."

"You are?" Peyton dropped her bag again. Her shoulders needed at least a few seconds of rest before she lugged it back up the steps.

"I wanted to give you this." Sawyer reached under the counter and extracted a book. "I know you were reading Dickens last time you were here. I'm sure you already have this one, but I saw it in a bookstore and thought of you, so . . ."

Peyton took the worn copy of *Oliver Twist* he passed her. Her face heated. He'd thought of her? Why? They barely knew each other.

She examined the book. Judging by its cover, it had to be old. She flipped to the copyright page. 1901. And it was in collectible condition. Which made it well beyond anything she could accept.

"Thank you." She held the book out to him. "But I can't take this. It's too much."

"For you, nothing's too much." Something warm lingered in Sawyer's look, and she felt her flush deepen.

"Okay, um." She glanced at the book again. "Thank you."

At his smile, she let herself give in to a smile, too. She couldn't deny that she loved the book.

"So, I was thinking ... I'm sure things are little awkward with you and Jared. Want to ditch the others and hit the slopes with me tomorrow?"

"Oh." Peyton's heart did a weird, unexpected skip. "I was going to spend the day by the fire reading." She held up the book as if for evidence.

"I don't know if anyone's told you this before, but you're at a ski lodge. You're supposed to ski." His blue eyes glinted, and she couldn't help but laugh.

"Yeah. If you remember, the first time I tried that I ended up with a broken wrist."

"That's because you didn't have the right teacher." He winked at her. "Come on, it'll be fun."

He smiled big enough to show a dimple in one cheek. She'd never noticed the dimple before. Then again, she'd never really looked at him before. She'd had eyes only for Jared.

But Jared was her past.

Maybe Sawyer was her future. Or at least her present.

"Okay." She worked to insert more certainty into her voice. "Yes. Let's do it."

Sawyer's dimple deepened. "Great. Nine o'clock. I'll pick you up at your room."

"Oh, that's okay, I'll meet you down here." A pinch of guilt pricked her stomach at the thought of Jared seeing her with Sawyer. But she pushed it aside. She had no reason to feel guilty.

She was about to grab her bag when she remembered what she'd come down here for in the first place. "Almost forgot. I need one more key for the girls' room."

"You got it." Sawyer's grin made her stomach somersault this time. It felt strange to have that reaction to a man who wasn't Jared. But also nice. Maybe this ski trip was what she needed to get over him after all.

Sawyer passed her the key with one last stomach-flipping smile, and she bent to pick up her bag.

As she yanked up on the strap, there was a loud ripping sound. The bag was suddenly too light as everything she'd packed spilled from the torn bottom to the floor.

She groaned. She'd known the bag wouldn't hold up much longer, but she hadn't had time to buy a new one before the trip. That's what she got for not planning ahead.

Face flaming, she slid her underwear under a pair of jeans as she pushed everything into a pile and tried to get her arms around it.

"I'll get it for you." Jared was striding across the lobby, wearing that same grim expression he'd worn every time they'd run into each other over the past year.

But Sawyer was already at her side, passing her a large canvas bag. "Here, use this."

She took it gratefully and shoved her clothing in first, then her books and makeup on top.

"Thanks." She glanced around to make sure she hadn't missed anything.

When she looked up, Sawyer held a hand out to her. She let him pull her to her feet, then reached for the bag.

But Sawyer got to it first, grabbing it with his left hand while his right still gripped hers. "I'll carry this up for you."

"That won't be necessary." Jared's voice cut in.

Peyton slid her hand out of Sawyer's. But she didn't miss the dark glare Jared shot his old friend.

"I'll take it." Jared reached to grab the bag from Sawyer, who seemed to size him up and then shrugged and held the bag out to him.

Sawyer touched a hand to Peyton's elbow. "I'll see you tomorrow morning, then. Nine o'clock."

He gave Jared a buddy slap on the back, then disappeared through the door behind the counter.

Jared started across the lobby with her stuff, and Peyton double-stepped to keep up. "Didn't you need something from the desk?"

"No." Jared's answer was short, clipped.

"Then why did you come down?" Peyton frowned. Even after they'd spent three years together, she sometimes didn't understand him.

"You'd been down here a long time. I wanted to make sure everything was okay." Jared didn't look at her as he said it.

She stopped in the middle of the stairway, crossing her arms in front of her. "You don't need to check up on me, Jared. I'm perfectly capable of taking care of myself."

"Clearly." Jared's dry tone made her grit her teeth.

He was not going to make her feel guilty for talking to another man. "What's that supposed to mean?"

"Nothing," Jared muttered.

"Fine." She jogged up the rest of the stairs and strode down the hallway ahead of him.

But halfway to her room, she stopped. "Actually, no. It's not fine. You didn't want to share your life with me. So you don't get to make me feel guilty about talking to someone who maybe does."

"Sawyer?" Jared scoffed. "He's only looking for a little fun for himself. He has no intention of sharing his life with you."

"Yeah?" Peyton felt the steam building. What right did he have to try to ruin her shot at happiness before it'd even started? "Is that why he gave me an early edition Dickens?"

Jared blanched at that, and Peyton felt a cold satisfaction pool in her stomach. Followed by a wave of guilt. But she pushed it away. Jared was the one who had brought Sawyer up.

He stopped in front of her. "I'm not trying to make you feel guilty, Peyton." His voice was quiet, almost tender, and she tried to steel herself against it. "Just be careful with Sawyer. He's not—" He cut off and pulled a hand through his hair. "He's not the kind of guy who's looking for a long-term relationship, if you know what I mean."

"Well, you'd know all about that wouldn't you?" Peyton jerked her bag out of Jared's hand. Her anger must have given her super-human strength because she barely noticed the bag's weight as she ran the rest of the way down the hall and shoved her key into the lock.

She let the door slam behind her.

Chapter 4

*J*ared's breath fogged in front of him as he stopped at the top of the ski hill, getting ready for another run. He'd been out here two hours already, and still his head wasn't any clearer than it had been yesterday. Seeing Peyton and Sawyer together had hardened the regret that had been swirling in his gut for the past year so that it sat there now, diamond hard and just as sharp.

"Hey. You been out here all morning?" Leah skied up next to him, cheerful as always.

He squinted into the glitter of the snow behind her and shrugged. "Only since the sun came up."

He'd been awake long before that, trying to shove aside the knot of fear that always clustered in his throat when he woke during the night. It'd taken too long to remember where he was. To remember that there hadn't been anything to be afraid of for a long time.

"You up for another run?" Leah peered down the slope. "Thought I was up for this blue trail, but it looks more intimidating than I remembered. They're sure it's intermediate?"

Jared offered a reassuring smile. "I'll go with you. But you'll be fine." Leah had always been pretty solid on her skis. Unlike Peyton, who had to stick to the green beginner slopes.

Jared started to pull his goggles down, but he caught a flash of white and pink jacket near the top of the chair lift. He turned his head to follow the chair as it crested the hill and the couple slid off, the man's hand on the woman's arm. On Peyton's arm.

It was the same way Jared had helped Peyton off the lift the first time they'd come here together. And she gave Sawyer the same smile she'd always given him.

The knot in Jared's gut pulled taut. Sawyer was not the kind of guy Peyton should be with.

Peyton glanced his way once, before her eyes went right back to Sawyer, who was gesturing toward the hill and seemed to be demonstrating the stance she should use. A shot of something hot and sharp that went beyond simple jealousy surged through him. What was Sawyer doing bringing her on this hill? It was way beyond her skill level.

"Ready?" Leah's voice tugged at him, but he couldn't tear his gaze away from Peyton.

"Maybe you should tell her to stick to the greens." He gestured toward Peyton with his chin.

"She's a big girl, Jared. She can make her own decisions about which hill to take."

Except he was sure taking this run hadn't been her decision. Sawyer had certainly goaded her into it.

He didn't know what angered him more: that Sawyer would put her at risk by taking her on a run she wasn't ready for or that she was so eager to impress him that she'd agree to it.

"Come on." This time Leah's command was insistent.

He pulled his eyes away from Peyton and slammed his goggles down. "Let's go."

The wind whipped at his cheeks as he let the swoosh of the snow under his skis take over his senses. For a minute, he let himself forget everything else and focus only on the spray of powdery snow around him, the next turn of his skis, the taste of the cold.

But he reached the runout at the base of the hill too soon, and as he slowed, he automatically turned to squint up the hill, seeking out Peyton.

There.

Halfway down the run, an expression of sheer terror on her face as she flew down the hill—way too fast. Jared scanned the terrain in front of her, on alert for dangers. He recognized Sawyer half a dozen yards ahead of her, looking over his shoulder with a yell of encouragement. What was that maniac doing? Didn't he know he had to watch out for Peyton? Sawyer practically lived on skis, but until four years ago, Peyton had never been on a ski hill in her life. That's why Jared had taken her on the beginner hill and had hung close the whole time, ready to jump in to help at the slightest sign of trouble.

Not that it'd done much good. He'd never forget her tears of pain when she fell and broke her wrist. She'd forgiven him instantly. Said there was nothing he could have done. But her pain had devastated him. He'd promised himself long ago that he'd never let another woman get hurt on his watch. And he'd failed the first woman he'd had the opportunity to keep safe.

Leah skidded to a stop next to him and followed his gaze. "You could just marry her, you know. Then you'd both be happy."

Jared turned away from the hill. "She seems plenty happy to me."

"Is she?" Leah jabbed her ski pole into the ground and gave him a hard stare. "Look, you know I love Peyton like a sister, and I love you, too. Clearly, you two are not over each other. But if you can't marry her and give her the life she deserves, then you need to let her go. Let her start again. It's not fair to her if you don't."

"I can't marry her, Leah." Jared pushed off, making his way toward the lift.

"Then you know what you need to do," Leah called from behind him.

Yeah, he did know what he had to do.

He just didn't know how to do it.

Chapter 5

"Again?" Sawyer shot Peyton the same impish grin he'd given her after every run so far.

Every muscle in her body ached, but she nodded, a return grin stretching her own cheeks. She was having way too much fun to quit.

Skiing with Jared had always been fun, too. But after she'd broken her wrist that first year, he'd hovered so much, always afraid to let her go too fast or get too far in front of him, in case she got hurt. It'd made her feel safe and protected. But it'd also kept her from experiencing the thrill of taking a hill at full speed.

Besides, she'd made more than a dozen runs already this morning, and she hadn't wiped out once. Clearly, Jared had underestimated her abilities. If it weren't for Sawyer, she would still be on the beginner slopes Jared had convinced her to stick to.

Sawyer grabbed Peyton's gloved hand as the chair lift swept under them. Of all the things Peyton missed about being in a relationship, holding hands was near the top of the list. Having her hand in another man's felt odd but not necessarily in a bad way.

"Want to grab some lunch after this?" Sawyer's grip tightened on hers. "We can go to one of the small reception areas that aren't being used. Have some privacy."

"Sure." To her surprise, Peyton didn't have to think about the answer. She'd had a nice morning with Sawyer and had even successfully managed to avoid watching Jared most of the time. Lunch with Sawyer—where Jared wouldn't be around to distract her at all—sounded nice.

"Race you down this time." He tugged her hand as they slid off the lift.

"You're on." She had to laugh at herself as she followed him. She never would have expected to enjoy his fun and fast style. But she felt fearless this morning.

Sawyer led her past the head of the blue trail they'd been taking all day to the edge of the hill, where the slope steepened sharply.

Peyton sucked in a breath as she caught a glimpse of the black diamond symbol on the sign off to the side. Was she really up for this advanced trail?

She shoved down the apprehension. If Sawyer thought she could handle it, then she was willing to give it a try. Besides, it was right next to the blue. How much harder could it be?

"Ready?" Sawyer winked at her, then lowered his goggles.

She blew out a quick breath, then pulled hers down and nodded.

"Set."

Peyton's shoulders tensed, and she tightened her grip on her poles, bending her knees so she'd be ready to push off.

"Go!"

At Sawyer's shout, Peyton shoved off, hard. Within seconds, she was flying down the hill, the snow biting at her cheeks. She angled her hips and crouched lower. She needed more speed if she was going to beat Sawyer.

Her heart thundered in her ears, cutting off all other sounds. The speed was exhilarating and terrifying at the same time. She wasn't sure she liked it, but she wasn't about to back off now. She'd started this challenge, and she was going to finish it.

Halfway down, she chanced a glance to the side. Sawyer was a few feet in front of her, but if she went a little faster, she might be able to catch him.

She let out an involuntary scream as she accelerated. She'd never gone this fast before outside of a vehicle. But she was gaining on him.

He looked back and shot her a smile, then started to inch ahead.

Oh, no, you don't.

She pushed her weight forward and concentrated on leaning her knees and ankles to the inside, the way Sawyer had explained. Her heart rate accelerated with the skis, and she let out a wild cackle. She was really doing this.

But just then her right ski caught an edge, and she felt her body jerk off balance.

Instinctively, she shifted her weight, but it was too late. Her feet were no longer under her. Her hip hit the ground first, then an explosion of pain shot through her ankle as her body twisted without her foot.

She laid still, trying to pull in a breath. But her lungs seemed to have frozen in place. She tried not to panic as she waited for them to start functioning again. Finally, she was able to gulp at the air, and she sat up, unable to hold back the moan as she reached for her foot. But before she could free it from her boot, the unmistakable zip of skis on the snow sounded above her. She whipped her head around to see a skier barreling toward her. There was no time to roll out of the way. She lifted her hands to cover her head and braced for the impact.

But only a gentle spray of powder landed on her, accompanied by the swish of skis skidding to a stop.

"Are you okay?"

She should have known it would be Jared. He'd been there to help every time she'd been hurt since they'd met. Including the day they met, when he'd rescued her from a rip current that had dragged her toward the breakwater the first time she'd ventured into Lake Michigan. She'd called him her hero then, and here he was again.

She uncovered her head and laid back in the snow. "It's my ankle."

"I've got it, man," Sawyer called, jogging up the hill in his ski boots.

But Jared was already releasing her foot from the ski and sliding off her boot. She sighed in relief as he lowered her foot to the snow but winced as his hands probed her ankle.

"I know," he soothed. "I need to check how bad it is."

"That was an awesome run." Sawyer dropped into the snow next to her, grinning. "You almost caught me."

Jared aimed a glare at Sawyer. "What were you thinking taking her on a black diamond?"

"What were you doing following us?" Sawyer shot back.

Peyton watched Jared, who didn't look up. Had he been following them?

"I've been on the black diamond for a couple hours now. I happened to see you guys head that way and thought I better keep an eye out. Good thing, too."

Sawyer waved him off. "She's fine. You always were a wimp about this kind of stuff."

Peyton's mouth fell open. The last thing she'd consider Jared was a wimp. Cautious, yes. But the man had run into burning buildings, for crying out loud.

Jared ignored Sawyer and continued to push on her ankle, drawing a sharp hiss when he pressed below it.

"I think it's just a sprain, but we'll keep an eye on it. You should get some ice on it right away."

"Does this count?" She gestured at the snow where her foot rested. She had no desire to get up and go anywhere else right now.

Jared gave her that gentle, easy laugh she used to love. "Afraid not. Come on. I'll help you to the lodge." He squatted at her side and reached to put a hand behind her back.

Sawyer jumped to his feet. "*I'll* help her. We were about to grab some lunch anyway."

Peyton hated the look on Jared's face. Hated that she'd put it there.

But there was nothing she could do about it. He'd chosen this for them.

"Thanks." She gave him a quick smile before accepting the hand Sawyer held out to her.

Jared turned away as Sawyer draped her arm over his shoulder and wrapped his arm firmly around her back.

"Try not to put any pressure on it." Jared called behind them as she hobbled next to Sawyer.

She nodded but resisted the urge to look over her shoulder at him.

By the time they got inside, her ankle was throbbing so hard she could feel her pulse in her whole foot.

"I think I need to sit," she managed to puff to Sawyer.

He steered her to the sunken couches around the fireplace and settled her in, tucking a pillow under her foot.

"I'll go grab you some ice."

Peyton laid back against the couch, closing her eyes. How did she always manage to get herself into these situations? Her mom was the most elegant person she knew, but her dad had always teased that gracefulness skipped a generation. Then he had tweaked her cheek and said her clumsiness was part of what made her so endearing.

She sighed. Maybe it would endear her to Sawyer. It had apparently worked with Jared. He'd come to check on her a few days after he'd saved her life, and they'd gotten to talking. Before they knew it, they were dating seriously.

And look what came of that.

"Here we go."

She opened her eyes as Sawyer passed her an ice pack.

A stab of pain sliced through her foot as she settled the ice onto it, but after a second the throbbing eased.

Sawyer passed her a sandwich and a soda. "Figured I might have to take a rain check on our private lunch. How about dinner instead?"

Peyton ran her hand down the cool side of the soda can. "I don't know." She liked Sawyer, but her insides churned with guilt over the way Jared had looked as she'd walked away with Sawyer's arm around her.

Sawyer settled on the low table in front of the couch. "Come on, it's just dinner." His phone rang, but he clicked it off, leaning forward and bracing his elbows on his knees, as if nothing in the world mattered more to him than her answer.

No was on the tip of her tongue. But the whole point of coming here was to move on. "Okay. Dinner it is."

"Great." Sawyer tucked a loose hair behind her ear.

The move that had felt so familiar whenever Jared did it caused an uncomfortable prickle in her belly. She wasn't quite ready to have Sawyer touching her hair like that.

But he was only being friendly.

She forced a smile as he waved and walked away.

She was still trying to sort out her feelings about the idea of spending time with a new man when Leah charged into the seating area a few minutes later.

"Are you okay?" Her friend's cheeks were pink-tinged, and snow crusted her hat. She must have come straight from the slopes.

"I'm fine." Peyton gestured to her foot. "Aside from a serious lack of grace and a terrible habit of demonstrating my clumsiness in front of a man."

Leah dropped to the couch next to her and leaned over to give her a hug. "I'm sorry I wasn't there. I decided to try the blues on the back side of the hill for a bit. They're a little tamer."

"That's okay. Sawyer was there." She hesitated a second. "And Jared."

"Yeah, he found me and sent me in here. He said it was sprained?"

Peyton tried to ignore the warm glow that came from knowing Jared had been worried enough to send Leah to check on her. And the pang that he hadn't come himself. "He's the expert, so I guess so. He said we'd have to keep an eye on it, but I think the ice is helping already."

"That's a relief. Remember how long the drive to the hospital is?"

Peyton groaned. "That was the longest car ride of my life."

"Your life? I was the one trapped in the car with you and Jared, listening to him apologize a bajillion times and you tell him it wasn't his fault a bajillion and one times." She broke off and covered her mouth with a hand. "I'm sorry. That was a dumb thing to say."

Peyton shook her head. "No, it's okay. Anyway, at least he doesn't blame himself this time. Pretty sure he blames Sawyer, though."

Leah's forehead creased. "Did Sawyer do something to make you fall?"

"No." Peyton leaned forward to pull off the ice, examining her ankle. It had turned an ugly purple-black and was definitely puffy. She hoped Jared was right about it only being a sprain. "He doesn't think I should have been on that hill in the first place. If it was up to him, I'd stay on the bunny hill the rest of my life."

"Well." Leah leaned back against the seat and kicked her feet up onto the table Sawyer had been sitting on a few minutes ago. "There are worse traits in a guy than wanting to keep you safe."

"Yeah. Like not wanting to get married." The bitter words were out before Peyton could hold them back. But she didn't want to talk about Jared anymore. "Anyway, I'm having dinner with Sawyer tonight."

Instead of the triumphant look she expected from her friend, Leah gathered her long hair into a ponytail with her hands, then let it fall.

Peyton knew Leah well enough to recognize that the gesture meant she had something to say but didn't want to say it. "Out with it."

Leah's eyebrows drew together. "I don't know if you should be hanging out with Sawyer."

Peyton stared at her friend. "Why not? Aren't you the one who's been trying to get me to move on?"

"I know." Leah played with the zipper of her jacket. "But Jared doesn't think Sawyer is the best guy when it comes to women."

Peyton snorted. "There's a surprise. He doesn't want to be with me, but he doesn't want anyone else to be with me either."

Leah shook her head. "I know, so I'm trying to take what he said with a grain of salt. But maybe it'd be best if you hung out with Sawyer in a group first."

Peyton couldn't stop the eye roll. "Yeah, because that wouldn't be awkward, trying to talk to Sawyer with Jared hanging over our shoulders."

"I'm sure Jared wouldn't—" Leah stopped. Considered. "Okay, yeah, he would. But that might be better than being alone with Sawyer until you know him better."

"And how am I supposed to get to know him better if I don't get a chance to talk to him alone?"

Why was Leah making such a big deal about this? Sawyer was one of the most charming men Peyton had ever met. It's not like he was going to attack her.

Leah shrugged. "I don't know. I guess in high school Sawyer had kind of a reputation for going through girls pretty quickly."

"High school was a long time ago, Leah. And I don't know that Sawyer. I only know this guy who bought me a book he knew I'd like and who took me out on the slopes and showed me what I was capable of. Now he wants to have a nice quiet dinner with me where we can talk without worrying about my ex being right there. Sounds like a good guy to me."

Leah's forehead was still creased, but she nodded. "I know, Peyton. I just want you to be safe."

Peyton patted Leah's leg. "I know you do, and I love you for it. But I'll be fine."

Better than fine, maybe. If having dinner with Sawyer could help her forget about Jared for even a couple hours, it would be worth it.

So far, nothing else had worked.

Chapter 6

Jared had told himself that the next run would be his last of the day at least five times already. But every time he got to the bottom of the slope, he considered the alternative: go inside and see Sawyer and Peyton together.

No, thank you.

He really did have to make this his last run, though, or he would miss dinner with his friends.

The line for the chair lift was still plenty long, and Jared fiddled with the small chain Peyton had given him for their first Valentine's Day as he waited. At first, he'd thought it was weird. Why would he want to wear a necklace? But now it had become a part of him. So much so that he couldn't bring himself to take it off.

"Excuse me." The woman in front of him turned, long dark hair poking out from under her hat to frame her face. "Do you know what time it is?"

"Sure." Jared dug into his zippered jacket pocket and pulled out his phone. "It's almost six."

"Thanks." She gave him a friendly smile.

"Sure."

"I'm April, by the way." She held out a hand and delivered another smile.

He shook it, letting himself smile back. "Jared."

"That last run of yours was pretty amazing."

Jared lifted his head. She'd been watching him? "Uh, thanks."

He gestured ahead of her, where the line had moved forward, leaving a large gap between her and the group in front of them.

She moved up to fill the gap, then angled back to him. "You want to take the next one together?"

Jared blinked at her. Was she flirting with him? It'd been so long since he'd had to decipher any woman's actions besides Peyton's. And she'd always been so easy to read.

"I was going to— I mean it's my last run, so—" Why was he so tongue-tied all at once?

"So?" She raised an eyebrow. "Make your last run with me. Or are you afraid you can't keep up?"

Jared laughed. She was spirited, that was for sure.

"I'll take that as a yes." She glided ahead again.

Jared followed more slowly. What had he just agreed to?

Dude, it's just skiing. Chill.

He skied up to the lift right behind April. On a whim, he grabbed her hand as they sat. She looked over and smiled.

But the hand in his felt wrong, and he let go as soon as their feet left the ground.

"So where are you from?" April's voice had an easiness to it that Jared wished he could imitate.

"You've probably never heard of it."

"Try me."

"Hope Springs. It's a little town on Lake Michigan, just—"

"You're kidding." April shoved his arm. "My grandma lives there. I love it. That little ice cream shop with the weird name. The Chocolate something. Chocolate Cow?"

"Chocolate Chicken." Jared chuckled. "Don't ask how it got its name. No one knows. Or if they do, they're not telling."

April laughed—probably harder than the comment deserved, but Jared grinned. He couldn't deny that her attention was nice.

They were still talking about Hope Springs when the lift reached the top of the hill. Jared followed April to the start of the black diamond Peyton had gotten hurt on earlier.

"You good for this hill?" he shouted at her back. He hadn't seen her ski yet, and he didn't want another person to get hurt on his watch today.

"Just try to keep up," she called over her shoulder as she pushed off.

Jared shoved off right behind her. After watching her for a second, he relaxed. This obviously wasn't her first time on the slopes. Her technique was flawless as she carved perfect curves down the hill.

By the time he reached the runout, she was standing and watching him, her hat in her hand, a mischievous spark in her eyes.

"Couldn't quite keep up, huh?" She shoved his shoulder playfully.

Jared rubbed his arm, pretending to be hurt. "Hey, let a guy keep some of his pride."

She raised her hands to her sides. "Fine. But I think it's only fair that you buy me dinner since I won."

Jared snickered. "I don't remember there being any wager. Or an official race."

"Okay, then, you can buy me an unofficial dinner."

Jared realized with a start that she was serious. She wanted to have dinner with him.

He should say no. He was supposed to have dinner with the whole group. And he should check on Peyton's ankle. And he shouldn't be having dinner with another woman.

"Come on." She nudged him again. "I want to talk more about Hope Springs. Maybe I'll plan a visit there soon." Her amber eyes were warm and bright, and he found that he didn't want to say no.

"Okay. Let me just go change." He pushed the door to the lodge open and held it for her. "Meet me in the dining area in half an hour?"

"Deal." She grabbed his hand for a quick squeeze, then flounced across the lobby and disappeared down the hallway to the right.

Jared crossed the large room more slowly. What was he thinking?

Peyton would be in the dining room. She'd see him with April. Much as he knew they both needed to move on, he didn't want to hurt her by showing up with another woman.

He stopped at the bottom of the staircase. As soon as he got to his room, he'd call April to cancel dinner.

Except he had no idea what room she was in.

He jogged toward the hallway she'd disappeared down, but it was empty, aside from a middle-aged man who shot him a suspicious glare.

Jared turned around and made his way up the stairs and to his room. When he got to the dining room, he'd just have to tell April he couldn't have dinner. It'd be awkward, but there was nothing that could be done about that.

Decision made, he knocked on the door to the girls' room. Before he did anything else, he needed to check on Peyton's ankle. If it was worse, he wouldn't be going to dinner with anyone. He'd be driving her to the hospital for an x-ray.

Sophie pulled the door open. "Hey, Jared. We were beginning to think you were going to spend the night on the hill."

He grinned. That sounded pretty good, actually. "Nah. Thought I better come in and check on my patient. How's she doing?"

"Better, I think. I actually haven't seen her. Spencer and I spent most of the day in town. We found this cute little antique store that Vi would love—" She broke off. "What's wrong?"

"You haven't seen her? Where is she?"

Sophie bit her lip. "I think Leah said something about dinner."

"With Sawyer?" Jared's jaw clenched. He'd told Leah to warn her about that guy.

Sophie touched a hand to his arm. "I think so."

"I guess I'll check her ankle later then." His voice was stiff, and he made himself gentle his tone. Sophie wasn't the target of his anger. "Thanks, Soph. Glad you and Spencer had a good day."

"You coming to dinner with us?"

He shook his head, a sudden decisiveness taking over. "Actually, no. I have other plans."

Chapter 7

"That was the best meal I've ever eaten." Peyton wiped her mouth and set her napkin on her plate.

Sawyer had gone all-out for dinner, ordering them ravioli in a white truffle sauce and a chocolate cherry cheesecake so decadent she was pretty sure it should be illegal. The meal, combined with the intimate reception room, with its widely scattered tables—all empty aside from theirs—and tasteful crystal chandeliers, had her feeling almost like a princess. She'd nearly forgotten about the throbbing in her foot.

"I'm glad you enjoyed it." The two candles that lit their table cast a soft glow on Sawyer's face, and the butterflies Peyton had finally managed to calm as she ate returned with a vengeance.

Being with Jared had become so familiar and comfortable, she wasn't used to this nervousness that kept her constantly off balance.

Sawyer's gaze on her was a little too intense, and she let her eyes travel to the full wall of windows so she'd have a moment to catch her breath. Moonlight glinted off the snow on the trees that covered the hill behind the lodge. Their shadows crisscrossed the ground in an intricate patchwork.

"Stunning, isn't it?" Sawyer's voice drew her eyes back to him. But he wasn't looking out the window. He reached his hands across the table and cupped them around hers.

She felt the heat rise in her cheeks as the butterflies took off at full speed. "It's beautiful here. You live here year-round now, right? What's it like in the summer?"

She was babbling, she knew it. But she needed to slow things down. She liked Sawyer. He seemed to be a nice guy. But she barely knew him. She gently slid her hands out from under his and pretended to adjust the sleeve of her shirt.

A frown puckered Sawyer's face for half a second, but he quickly erased it and gave her an easy smile. "It's even more beautiful, if you can believe it. Wildflowers everywhere. Everything's green and lush. The deer come right up to this window sometimes."

"Wow. That does sound beautiful." This was better. Talking about safe things. Taking it a little slower. Sawyer was the first guy she'd done so much as have a meal with since she and Jared broke up, unless you counted Ethan and Spencer, who were both in happy relationships. She needed to get the feel for this dating thing again before she jumped right in.

"We see deer in winter, too. But they stay closer to the woods. Actually, this is usually about the time they come out. " He swiveled in his chair to peer out the window. "Yep. Two of them. Right over there."

He pointed, and Peyton squinted out the window. "I don't see anything."

"Right at the edge of the tree line."

But all she saw was more trees.

Sawyer pushed his chair back and came to stand behind her. He bent until his face was almost pressed against hers and raised his hand to point again. She tried to follow the line of his finger, but she was too aware of his nearness.

"Where?" Her voice sounded scratchy and unnatural.

He used his hands to turn her head, grazing a thumb across her cheek, then let his arm fall across her shoulders. She tried not to tense as she peered into the darkness. But her heart was beating too fast, and she felt that same mix of exhilaration and terror she'd felt on the ski hill right before she'd crashed.

Finally, she picked out two shapes moving against the silhouette of the trees. "I see them."

The deer were nosing through the snow, seemingly oblivious that they had an audience.

She waited for Sawyer to lift his arm off her and move back to his seat.

But he pressed closer and inhaled deeply. "You smell nice."

"Thanks," she managed to get out. But she needed space.

Right now.

She stood abruptly, and he grabbed the chair to keep from losing his balance.

She limped to the window, pretending to strain for a better look at the deer as she drew in a few calming breaths. Now that she was on her feet, her ankle set to throbbing again, but she ignored the pain.

In the window's reflection, she saw Sawyer move to blow out the candles on the table.

Now she felt bad. She was letting Jared's stupid warning about Sawyer prejudice her feelings about him.

He'd done nothing wrong. He just wanted to show her that he liked her.

And she liked him, too.

"I'm sorry." She turned toward him and made herself meet his eyes. "I didn't mean to push you away. I just need to move a little more slowly."

"Of course." His smile was charming and little-boyish at the same time, and she found herself smiling back.

She limped closer, and his expression dropped into a frown. "You shouldn't be on your feet. How about a movie?"

"I don't think there's one playing tonight." She'd checked the schedule for the lodge's small theater when they'd arrived as part of her plan to avoid Jared.

Sawyer winked. "There are some perks to owning the place, you know."

He held out his arm to her, and she took his elbow, letting him support her as they made their way to the theater.

She felt like a kid sneaking in somewhere she didn't belong as he held the door to the dark theater open for her, but she shoved the feeling aside. Sawyer's family owned the place. She wasn't doing anything wrong.

She pushed down the image of Jared glaring at Sawyer on the slopes. Pushed down the warning he'd made Leah deliver to her. Sawyer was a good guy. She was perfectly safe with him. Jared was just being overbearing, as usual.

"Be right back." Sawyer gave her shoulder a gentle squeeze as he led her to a row of seats on the far side of the theater, then disappeared into the projector room.

Peyton settled in and tried to relax. She wouldn't give Jared another thought tonight.

Chapter 8

Jared held the lodge door open and waited for April to pass through. When he'd met up with her earlier, she'd suggested that they skip the dining room in favor of a pizza place she knew in town, and Jared had jumped at the offer. He couldn't stand the thought of spending another minute in the building where Sawyer was working his charms on Peyton.

"Thanks for dinner." April stopped inside the doors. "Maybe we can do it again tomorrow?"

Jared ran his hand back and forth on his chin. Dinner had been nice enough, but he'd known halfway through that he and April would never work. It wasn't her—she was funny and kind and vivacious. But she wasn't Peyton.

Not that he had any idea how to tell her that. "I'm sorry. I just—"

But she held up a hand to stop him. "I kind of had a feeling. For what it's worth, I hope you patch things up with Peyton."

He chuckled wryly. Had he really talked about Peyton that much? "I'm sorry, I didn't mean to—"

But she dropped a hand onto his arm. "It was sweet, actually. She's a very lucky woman to have someone who loves her so much."

Somehow, he didn't think Peyton would see it that way.

"Anyway, maybe I'll run into you in Hope Springs sometime. My grandma's always bugging me to visit more." She gave that sparkling laugh of hers again, squeezed his forearm, and bounded across the lobby.

Jared shook his head and scrubbed his hands over his face. What was he thinking, letting a woman like that walk away in exchange for something that would never happen?

But he'd realized at dinner that if he couldn't be with Peyton, he didn't really want to be with anyone. At least not right now. Maybe never.

He trudged across the lobby, up the staircase, and through the empty hall toward his room.

He should check on Peyton's ankle, but he had no desire to hear her gushing about Sawyer to the other girls. He could check it in the morning.

But a stab of conscience stopped him as he was about to unlock his own door.

She could be in pain or need more advanced medical attention. She'd trusted him with her care, and he owed it to her to follow up.

With a sigh, he shoved his key into his pocket and crossed the hall to knock on the girls' door.

Leah pulled it open, and her face fell into a frown. "I thought you were Emma. She ran downstairs to grab some ice cream. Want to join us?"

"Where's Peyton?"

Leah shook her head. "You know where she is, Jared."

"She's not back yet?" Jared shoved the door open and looked past Leah. Sophie and Ariana waved from across the room, where they were playing some game at the table.

"Relax." Leah stood aside so he could come in. "She texted a while ago to say they were going to watch a movie."

Jared's hands clenched. "Where?" The theater had been closed when he walked past it downstairs. "If he took her to his room—"

"You know her better than that, Jared." Leah's voice was sharper than he'd ever heard it. "Sawyer opened up the theater for a private screening."

"So she's alone with him?" He clenched his teeth so hard pain shot up his jaw. If that guy laid a hand on her, so help him. "You were supposed to warn her."

"I did." Leah eyed him with a mix of pity and compassion. "But you can understand how she thought your assessment might be a little biased."

Jared blew out a breath. He supposed it might be. But it wasn't jealousy that had motivated him to tell Leah to keep Peyton away from Sawyer. Or at least, not only jealousy. He'd heard Sawyer tell one too many stories to feel comfortable with him being alone with any woman he knew. Especially one as open and trusting as Peyton.

"She has her phone on her, Jared. She'll let me know if anything is wrong."

Jared spun on his heel and stalked down the hall.

"Where are you going?" Footsteps shuffled across the carpet behind him, and the girls' door banged shut as

Leah grabbed his elbow. "Don't go after her, Jared. It's not fair. To either of you."

"I just have to see that she's okay."

Leah gathered her hair at the base of her neck. "Jared, she's fine. She said she was having a really good time." She dropped her hair and laid a hand on his arm. "I'm sorry."

Jared pulled both hands through his hair and locked his fingers behind his head, pacing the short width of the hallway. "So I'm supposed to, what— Stand by and watch her go out with him?"

Leah gave him a sad smile. "Yeah. Unless you're going to change your mind and give her the life she wants, that's exactly what you're supposed to do."

Jared dropped his arms, gave Leah one last look, then strode down the hallway.

"Jared, don't." But this time Leah didn't follow him.

"I'm not," he called over his shoulder. "I just need to go for a walk."

"Where? It's late."

He raised his hands to his sides. "Doesn't matter where."

"At least let one of us come with you."

Jared shook his head and kept walking. He knew his friends would do anything for him.

But right now the only thing he needed them to do was leave him alone.

Chapter 9

*P*eyton tried to make herself relax. Sawyer had chosen *When Harry Met Sally*, one of her all-time favorite movies. But she couldn't concentrate on it with his arm around her. Couldn't get used to the way he was running his hand up and down her shoulder. She shifted on the double seat to put a little more distance between them, but he shifted with her, moving so that his head rested on hers.

He nuzzled his face into her hair. "You smell so good."

"So you said." She tried to keep things light. Maybe Sawyer hadn't understood what she'd meant by taking things slowly.

Then again, he was just smelling her hair.

She forced herself to take a slow breath and unclench her fists.

Sawyer wrapped a hand around hers and lowered his mouth to her neck, dusting a light kiss there.

Peyton reared back, jerking her head away. Her pulse pounded against her temple. She suddenly didn't want to be here anymore.

She half stood, waiting for Sawyer to move so she could get to the aisle. But he grabbed her hand, pulling her down next to him.

Her heart thundered harder, and the impulse to run seized her.

But Sawyer slid a gentle hand along her cheek. "Relax. You don't think I would hurt you, do you?"

She tried to get her heart rate under control. Of course he wouldn't hurt her. She was overreacting.

"Sorry. I'm not used to—"

"I know." His hand slid from her cheek into her hair. "I'm sorry if I'm moving too fast. You're just so beautiful."

He leaned closer, tilting his head down toward hers, and his eyes fell closed.

Peyton closed her eyes, too, telling herself this was what she wanted. She hadn't been kissed in almost a year.

But the moment their lips touched, she knew it wasn't right. His lips were not the ones she wanted to feel.

She pulled back as gently as she could.

Sawyer's eyes remained closed for a second longer, then he straightened. When he opened his eyes, something dark flashed in them for a second, but it was gone so quickly Peyton was sure she'd imagined it.

"I'm sorry." She set a hand on his arm, then drew it back, locking her fingers together in her lap. "I don't think I can—"

"It's okay." Sawyer blew out a breath. "Is this about Jared?"

"No." But if he had even a fragment of skill in reading people, he'd know that was untrue. When Sawyer had kissed her, all she could think was that he wasn't Jared. "I mean, it's complicated—"

"What's complicated?" He gripped her hands. "I like you. I think you like me. Jared has nothing to do with anything anymore."

She nodded. Of course he was right. Jared shouldn't have any bearing on anything she did.

His grip on her hands loosened, and he moved closer, sliding his hands up her arms. "That's better. Now let's try this again."

Before she'd figured out what he meant by "this," he'd wrapped both arms around her back and was pressing his lips to hers.

She gasped in a sharp breath and tried to slide away, but he squeezed her tighter, his mouth moving hungrily against hers. Nothing about it felt sweet or warm or right.

Blood pounded in her ears as she raised her hands to his chest and pushed. But he was bigger than her and had her wrapped too firmly.

"Please," she gasped around his mouth. "Stop."

He pulled his head back and loosened his grip slightly. "What's wrong?"

"I just— I want to go back to my room—" She tried to wriggle free from his grasp, but his arms didn't budge.

He gave her a slow smile. "That sounds nice. But we're alone here. No one's going to disturb us."

Fear clawed at her lungs. That wasn't what she'd meant.

"No, I—" She struggled harder.

But he was already leaning closer, bringing his mouth toward hers.

She gave a hard shove against his chest and screamed the only word she could think of in that moment.

"Jared!"

Chapter 10

*J*ared jolted upright and swiveled his head to search the lobby. It was empty, aside from an older couple snuggling in front of the fire. But he could have sworn he heard something.

He was probably going crazy from sitting here so long.

After walking the grounds for an hour, he'd been frozen through, but he hadn't been able to face going up to his room, so he'd planted himself in the lobby. He couldn't help it that the comfortable seat he'd chosen happened to be tucked into a nook near the theater. Or that he had a view of the theater doors if he leaned out and craned his neck. Which he'd found himself doing.

Frequently.

He glanced at the oversize clock on the opposite wall. He'd been here for forty minutes already. Surely their movie would be done soon, and they'd come out. He'd see that Peyton was safe, and everything would be fine.

He tried not to imagine what else they might be doing in there besides watching the movie. He knew Peyton intended to wait for marriage.

But that didn't mean she was immune to Sawyer's charms.

Jared jumped to his feet and started toward the theater doors.

But halfway there he drew up short. Leah was right. He had no business interfering. He should go to bed.

He turned toward the steps, but a sound stopped him.

This time he was sure he heard it. A shout of some sort.

He swiveled to search the lobby again. But the couple by the fire were laughing, and the desk clerk was typing on the computer.

Anyway, it had sounded like it came from behind him.

From the theater.

He spun and rushed the door, not letting himself pause to think. He charged inside but drew up short at the sudden darkness.

"Sawyer, please!" That was definitely Peyton's voice.

Jared's heart lurched, and he stumbled forward, not caring when he bashed his leg against the back of a seat.

His pulse drummed in his ears as his eyes swept the empty seats.

There.

Sawyer had his arms wrapped around Peyton, his face lowered to hers.

Jared froze. Everything in him went numb. Nothing could have prepared him for seeing Peyton kissing another man.

But she jerked her head back. "Stop!"

Her scream shot him across the room as a boiling rage took over.

In two seconds flat, his grip was locked on Sawyer's shirt, and he yanked him into the aisle.

He pulled his fist back and drove it into Sawyer's cheekbone.

Sawyer staggered to the side, grabbing his face and swearing. "What the— Who do you think you are?"

But Jared ignored him and turned to Peyton. She was white and shaking.

He held a hand out to her. "You okay?" His voice was gruff and barely controlled.

She nodded but then screamed as a hand fell on his shoulder and spun him around. He knew what was coming, and he knew what he had to do.

The punch landed against his eye socket, shooting fireworks through his skull. But he shook off the pain. He'd dealt with worse than that.

He pivoted on his rear leg, putting all his force into the reverse punch that smashed into Sawyer's nose, followed by a swift hook to his jaw.

Sawyer doubled over, lifting a hand to staunch the flow of blood from his nose.

"You will never touch her again." All the rage Jared had ever felt for his father, for any man who would hurt a woman, spiked his words.

He grabbed Peyton's hand and pulled her out of the seats. She clutched at his hand as he led her down the aisle, but she kept stumbling.

He stopped and swept an arm under her knees to pick her up.

She hissed in a breath but didn't protest.

Neither of them said a word as he carried her out of the theater and across the lobby.

"I can walk," she finally said at the base of the staircase.

He set her down. But he couldn't look at her.

Now she knew the real him. Knew the anger he was capable of feeling. The hurt he was capable of inflicting.

The silence stretched as they made their way slowly up the stairs. She was limping pretty badly, but she kept climbing, her breaths coming in short puffs.

When they reached their rooms, he made himself look at her. She was studying the key in her hand.

"I should check your ankle."

"It's fine." She shoved her key in the lock.

He started to protest, then closed his mouth.

After seeing that he could use his hands for far more than healing, she probably wanted to get as far away from him as possible.

And he didn't blame her one bit.

Look at the bright side. He stuck his own key into the lock. *At least now she won't want to marry you anymore.*

Some bright side.

Chapter 11

If it was possible, Peyton's eyes were heavier now than they'd been when she'd finally dropped into an uneasy sleep an hour before dawn. She groaned as she pushed the covers off herself. She'd spent most of the night reliving the paralyzing helplessness that had washed over her when Sawyer refused to stop kissing her. The relief she'd felt when Jared burst into the theater looking ready to burn down any obstacle to get to her. The anger she'd felt at herself for not listening to his warning in the first place.

But she'd wanted so badly to believe that Sawyer was the answer to her prayers for a future.

She scowled at herself in the mirror as she limped toward the bathroom. The others had already gone down to breakfast, but she'd pleaded a headache and said she'd meet them in the lobby so they could go to church together. Usually, Sundays were her favorite day of the trip. She loved the little country church they attended, with the friendly locals. Loved the little diner they always went to for lunch. Loved the park next to it where they'd had more than one snowball fight.

But today the thought of all that left a sour feeling in her stomach.

She stepped into the shower, trying to let the hot water wash away her memories. But it only seemed to amplify them.

Not only memories of last night. But memories of all the beautiful moments she'd shared with Jared. Of how he'd always made her feel safe. Of how he'd told her he couldn't marry her.

Why not, Lord? Why isn't the future I want happening for me?

Her tears mingled with the spray from the shower. Didn't God see that she needed some divine intervention here? She was trying so hard to find a husband and a family and the life she'd always wanted. So why wasn't it happening?

By the time she got out of the shower, she had five minutes to finish getting ready before she had to meet the others. She threw on her clothes, swiped on some eye makeup to hide the puffiness and dark circles, then hobbled out the door as quickly as she could, wincing with each step.

Halfway down the staircase, a sudden trembling took over her legs. What if Sawyer was at the desk? What if he approached her?

She tried to ignore the shakiness and keep going, but her legs refused to carry her down another step.

She stood, frozen.

"Peyton." Leah's relieved cry from the bottom of the staircase drew her eyes, and before she could move another inch, her friend had run up the steps and engulfed her in a hug. "Jared told us what happened. Are you okay?"

She nodded even as tears pricked at her eyelids again.

Leah wrapped an arm around her and led her toward the rest of the group, gathered in the sunken area around the fireplace. She started to breathe easier.

Until she caught sight of Jared.

A vicious purple and green bruise surrounded his eye, which was almost swollen shut.

He stood with the others but refused to look at her.

She didn't blame him. What must he think of her after what he had seen last night?

Had she even thanked him for coming to her rescue? Everything was such a blur she couldn't remember.

"I've already let the desk clerk know we'll be checking out today," Ethan said in a low voice. "We'll leave it up to you if we go to church first or just head out right away."

"Oh, we don't have to leave." Peyton was touched, but there was no way she was going to let Sawyer ruin their whole vacation.

"We're leaving." Jared's voice was hard, brooking no arguments.

Leah gave him a look, then turned to her. "Do you still want to go to church?"

"Yeah. I'd like that."

She tried to ignore Jared's grimace. She hadn't seen him in church since they'd broken up, but he'd just have to deal with it. She needed the reassurance of God's love right about now.

They moved as a group toward the door, her friends surrounding her like a human shield. As they crossed the parking lot, Peyton tried to maneuver closer to Jared so she could thank him. But every time she got near him, he skirted away.

Then they were in the van and she was pressed between Leah and Ariana, who seemed determined to keep her distracted.

But once they were seated in church, there was nothing to keep Peyton's mind from wandering to last night. What would have happened if Jared hadn't come in? Would Sawyer have tried to do more?

A shudder passed through her, and Leah reached over to squeeze her hand. Peyton squeezed back gratefully, then bowed her head, trying to pray as she waited for the service to begin.

But she had poured out everything she had in the shower this morning. So she sat quietly and waited for God to calm her spirit as he had so many times in her life.

She didn't understand why she felt more agitated than ever by the time the service started. The calming words of the hymns only stirred her up more, until she felt a restless need to move. She bounced her leg and twisted her hands in her lap. Leah shot her a raised eyebrow. Peyton sat on her hands and tried to still her legs.

But as the pastor stood to deliver his message, she felt the need to move again.

Until he started talking.

"Have you ever felt like God doesn't know what he's doing with your life?" The pastor sounded as if he were having a conversation with a friend.

Peyton fell dead still. Was he talking directly to her?

"Sure," the pastor continued, "you trust that he's in control. But you think he's making a mess of everything."

Peyton leaned forward in her seat, mouth open. That's exactly how she felt. She'd prayed over and over and over again for a husband who would love her the way her parents loved each other. And God had given her that man in Jared. But he wasn't willing to be her husband. And then, yesterday, she'd thought God had sent her another man. Another chance.

Wrong again.

So what was she supposed to do next?

Peyton forced her attention back to the sermon. The pastor was telling a story from his own life. Something about how he'd wanted to be a baseball player. He'd even made it to the minor leagues. And just when he was on the cusp of his big break, he'd been in an accident that had destroyed his shoulder.

"Let me tell you, I railed at God about that. I told him, I said, 'God, next time maybe you should check on what my future is going to be before you go letting me waste my time on something that's never going to pan out.' Can you imagine talking to God that way?"

Peyton dropped her gaze to her lap. She didn't have to imagine it. Hadn't she done the same thing a thousand times? *God, make sure the next one wants to marry me first.*

"And then I was so bold as to tell God what he should do with my life now that he'd messed it up. I said, well, if I can't be a baseball player, I want to be a coach. High school, college, pro, I didn't care. I applied for all these jobs. And each one came back: no, nope, no thank you. And I was devastated. Why was God blocking my plans at every turn?"

The pastor paused, and Peyton held her breath. That's what she wanted to know, too. Why did God keep stopping her plans? When would he start making things happen for her?

"And here's the thing I've finally realized." The pastor paused, looking at each person in turn. When his eyes fell on Peyton, she stilled. She could feel that whatever he said next was going to be the truth.

"I didn't see it at the time," he continued. "I was too busy resenting God. But now, I can see it. It's right there, in Jeremiah 29:11. God says, 'For I know the plans I have for you, plans to prosper you and not to harm you, plans to give you hope and a future.'"

The pastor spread his arms wide. "Do you see it?" He smiled as if he'd just delivered the greatest gift. "I was running after *my* plans. Not God's. And that was about the dumbest thing I could do. Who was I to think that I knew what was best for my future? God's plans are perfect. Why would I want anything less than that?"

Peyton sank back in her seat. Was that what she was doing? Running after her own plans instead of God's? Had she really thought she knew what she needed better than her heavenly father did?

Okay, Lord. The prayer flowed from her heart. *Help me to stop fighting your plans. Whatever they are, I know they are better than any plan I could come up with.*

She shifted in her seat. What if God's plans for her didn't include marriage and a family? What if they looked nothing like what she wanted so badly? *Help me to be content with the hope and the future you give me, even if it means remaining single.*

Simply praying the words pierced her heart, but as she stood to sing the next song, a stillness settled over her.

Trusting God with her future was right. No matter where he may lead her.

Chapter 12

*J*ared exhaled in relief. The church service was finally over.

He'd had to force himself to stay in his seat as the pastor had gone on and on about God's plans.

Where were God's plans when he was a kid? Was it God's plan for him to watch his dad beat his mom to within an inch of her life? Was it God's plan for his mom to walk out, leaving him alone with his dad? Was it God's plan to give him a past that guaranteed he couldn't have a future?

Because if those were God's plans, no thank you. He was doing just fine with his own plans.

What plans? To be alone and miserable the rest of your life?

He shoved the thought aside as he filed out of the pew behind the others. Alone and miserable was better than being with someone and constantly fearing he'd hurt them someday.

In the lobby, Peyton was having an enthusiastic conversation with the pastor. At least if she dated him, Jared probably wouldn't have to worry about her safety.

For the millionth time he kicked himself for letting her get into that situation with Sawyer yesterday. He should have done more than tell Leah to warn her. He should have warned her himself. Or barged in there sooner and dragged her away from Sawyer, whether she liked it or not.

Being the object of her fury would be better than being the one who had let her get hurt.

Again.

"I'll be in the van," he muttered to Leah.

He pushed out the church doors before she could answer. The others would catch up when they were ready. He couldn't stay in here a minute longer.

In the van, he leaned his head against the seat and let out a long breath. He couldn't wait to get home. To put this entire weekend behind him. To put Peyton behind him. Now that he knew she'd never look at him without seeing the monster he'd become last night, maybe she'd be easier to let go of.

The passenger door opened, but Jared didn't turn his head.

"Hey." It was Dan's voice. "How's the shiner? Need some ice?"

Jared shook his head. Pastor Boy here could go ahead and judge him for hitting Sawyer last night. He'd do it again a hundred times if it meant keeping Peyton safe.

"At least you didn't break anything. I got in a fight once in high school and broke my hand."

Jared turned his head a fraction, eying Dan.

"It was stupid." Dan chuckled lightly. "The kid was like twice my size. But he insulted my dad, and I kind of lost it. I aimed for his face, but he ducked and my hand ended up smashing into a locker."

"At least you had a dad worth defending," Jared muttered.

"Yeah." Dan sounded thoughtful. "I guess I never thought of it that way."

Funny how people who had good parents—parents who loved them—never really thought about it. What would his life have been like if he hadn't had to give his dad a thought?

"Anyway." Dan flipped on the heater. "Just remember that even if your earthly father is less than perfect, you have a heavenly father who loves you perfectly."

Jared nodded tightly. He knew Dan meant well. But for Dan the word father meant safety and love and acceptance. For Jared, it meant terror and loathing. So he didn't need two fathers. One was more than enough.

"Look, I know we don't know each other that well. But if you ever want to talk—"

"Here come the others." Jared jabbed at the buttons to open the back doors, and Dan fell silent.

Jared kept his focus on the steering wheel as the others climbed in so he wouldn't accidentally catch a glimpse of the fear he knew would hover in Peyton's eyes when she looked at him now.

"Let's eat. I'm starved." Leah tapped the back of his seat. "To the diner, driver."

Ten minutes later, Jared pulled the van into the already full diner parking lot.

He swallowed a groan. They'd be waiting here for at least an hour before they were seated.

"Should we skip it?"

But he already expected the variations of "no way" that sounded from the backseat.

"Peyton?" His eyes sought hers in the rearview mirror. Her opinion was the only one he cared about right now.

If she wanted to get out of here, he was going to take her home, no matter what the others wanted.

She met his eyes in the mirror for a second. "I think we should stay."

He sighed and ran a hand over his head.

Fine.

They'd eat and then they'd be on the road.

He pushed his door open and waited for the others to clamber out.

Peyton hung back as the rest of the group surged toward the door.

He gestured for her to go ahead of him, but she remained planted.

"Can we talk?" Her brow was furrowed into grooves, and she refused to look him in the eyes.

He'd known this was coming, but his heart shriveled anyway.

"Yeah, okay."

"How about the park?" She pointed to the tracked-up snow at the park next door as if he didn't know exactly where she meant.

He took stock of her leggings and sweater. "Won't you be cold?"

She gave a little laugh. "You worry about me too much."

He supposed he did at that. But he didn't know how not to. Especially after last night.

"At least let me help you walk there." He held out his arm, bracing for her refusal. But she wrapped her hand around his forearm, leaning her weight into him.

He tried not to let himself feel anything at her touch, but it was impossible not to notice the electricity of her hand on his arm.

"I should really check your ankle." If it was broken, she shouldn't be walking anywhere.

"It's a little better today."

He stole a glance at her. "Liar."

She puffed out a breath. "Forgot you could read me. But at least it isn't worse than it was yesterday. That's a good sign, right?"

"I'll feel better after I check it."

"Fine." She tightened her grip on his arm as they moved into the snow-covered grass. "You can check it when we sit down."

He led her to the closest picnic table and waited as she lowered herself onto it, her leg stretched to the side on the bench.

He sat carefully next to her foot, gently sliding the bottom of her legging up just enough to examine her ankle. It was still purple and bruised, but the swelling had gone down a bit. He set a hand lightly to the skin, careful not to apply too much pressure.

Finally, he was satisfied. "I'm going to stick with mild sprain. But you really have to stay off it for the next few days."

She waved a hand in the air. "I'm not going to be doing any more skiing, if that's what you mean. I was stupid to think I could handle that black diamond."

Jared shrugged, gazing toward the swings. "Sawyer should have known better."

The name sent a tension crackling through the air between them. They both fell silent.

Jared chanced a sideways look at her. Her face was turned away from him, and her lips were tipped into a deep frown. Was that how she would always look when she saw him now?

"Peyton, I—"

"Jared, about—"

They both stopped and laughed nervously, then fell silent again.

"You go first," he said after a minute.

"I just wanted to say, what you saw last night—" She stared at her hands in her lap. "I wasn't— I just don't want you to think—"

"I know."

She nodded and blinked quickly. "I should have listened to you. I shouldn't have let him—"

Jared shoved to his feet and moved to crouch in front of her. He grabbed her hands. "Hey. This is not your fault. This is all on Sawyer." Who deserved a lot worse than what he'd gotten.

"Okay?" He waited for her to look at him and nod, then squeezed her hands and returned to his spot at the far end of the bench.

She let out a long sigh, and he watched her. He needed to know she was going to be okay. She offered him a weak smile. But it wasn't enough to hide her shiver.

"See, you are cold. Let's get back to the diner." He stood to help her up, but she refused his hand.

"Not until you go."

"Go where?"

"You were about to say something before."

He wrapped a hand around the back of his neck. He didn't want to say it anymore. Not when things finally felt a little easier between them. But he had to.

He slipped off his jacket and held it out to her. She hesitated a moment, then took it and wrapped it around herself.

The sharp breeze sliced through Jared's dress shirt, but he didn't care.

"I just wanted to apologize for the way I reacted last night. I shouldn't have lost my temper like that. I'm sorry if I scared you." He focused on the spot where his toe was plowing a bare spot in the snow.

"Jared."

He'd thought he knew every tone of her voice, but this one he didn't recognize. It was enough to pull his eyes to hers. That pale blue drew him in. He took an involuntary step forward. She shifted so that her foot was on the ground, then grabbed his hand and tugged him to sit on the bench next to her.

"You didn't scare me. You *saved* me. I don't know what would have happened if—"

She broke off, and Jared's fists clenched. The thought of Peyton being hurt was too much.

"But the way I punched him. You weren't even a little scared to know I was capable of that? You weren't afraid I could do that to you?"

Peyton tilted her head toward her shoulder, studying him. "Jared, you are the person who makes me feel safest in the world. I know you would never hurt me."

Something broke in Jared, and he doubled forward, dropping his head into his hands. How could she trust him? How could she be so sure he would never do that?

But she didn't know how he was raised. Didn't know what his father had been capable of. What he'd passed on to Jared.

A soft hand fell on his back. "Where is this coming from?" Her voice was gentle, concerned. Inviting. But he shook his head. He couldn't tell her. Couldn't let her know about the true monster he was destined to become someday.

"Jared, please. Don't shut me out." Her whisper shot right through him, and he stood abruptly.

She thought she wanted to know?

Fine.

Maybe this was the final severing their relationship needed.

"You know how I don't talk to my dad and I don't see my mom? You want to know why that is?"

Hurt crossed Peyton's face. "You know I do. But you always refused to talk about it."

"That's because I didn't want to see the way you'd look at me. I didn't want you to be afraid of me."

"Afraid of you? Jared, I just told you I could never—"

He held up a hand. If he was going to tell her this, he had to do it now, before he took the coward's way out again.

"My dad beat my mom. Gave her bruises. Sometimes broke her bones. One time almost killed her."

Peyton's eyes widened, and she covered her mouth with both hands. He turned away. He didn't need to see her horror.

"I told my mom so many times to leave him. That we weren't safe. And she finally did." He sucked in a shaky breath. "Only she left me, too."

Peyton's gasp echoed across the empty park and stuck in his heart.

But he wasn't done yet. He hadn't told her the worst of it. "He hit me sometimes. Not as bad as he hit her. By then, I think he knew I was big enough to hit back." He swallowed, blinking back the memories. "Anyway, I moved out the day I graduated high school. And you know what my dad said to me that day? He said—" He made his voice gruff and hoarse, in an impression of his father. "'You think you're too good to turn out like your old man, son. But you wait and see. This is your future. Same as it was mine. Same as it was my father's. It's in our blood.'"

His breath came in short gasps at the memory. He'd been trying to forget it, trying to ignore it, trying to tell himself his dad was wrong his whole life. But deep down, he knew he was his father's son.

At least now Peyton knew. At least now he wouldn't have to be afraid of her finding out. Of what she'd think of him once she knew.

Even if it nearly killed him to realize how she must see him now.

"Oh, Jared." A pair of gentle arms wrapped around him from behind.

Every muscle in his body lost the tension that had been keeping him upright. He sagged and spun toward her, letting his arms go around her and ducking his head until it rested on hers.

A single sob tore lose from his middle, and her arms clutched him closer.

He stood there, just breathing. Slowly, a feeling of safety and peace descended on him. How could someone so small make him feel so protected?

After a few minutes, she pulled back, but she slid her hand into his and led him toward the bench. She pressed close to his side as they sat. After all he'd told her, what was she still doing here?

"You never told me." There was no accusation in her voice. More like . . . understanding.

"At least now you know why I can't marry. I have to break the cycle. I will not become my dad."

Peyton dropped her head to his shoulder, and he ached at the familiar move of trust.

"Whether you marry or not, Jared, you are not your father."

"But he said—"

"He was wrong. I know you. I know your heart. You would never hurt me or any other woman or child. You are a good man, Jared. You've made it your mission in life to help people who are hurt. Do you really think one day you're just going to switch that off and start hurting people?"

Jared shrugged.

"You know." Her voice was soft and sure at the same time. "I realized something in church this morning."

Jared tensed, but he found he wanted to know what she had to say, even if it was about church. "What's that?"

"I realized I thought I had my future all planned out and that God would just work things to match my plans." Her smile was tinged with sadness. "But much as we might want to plan our future, that's not what God calls us to do. And I think, you've been so sure all these years that your future was what your dad said it would be. But it's not, Jared. That is not God's plan for you."

He wanted to believe it. "How can you be so sure?"

"Because—" She locked her fingers with his. "You have another father, too, Jared, and he has made you into the most incredible man I know. He used all those awful, awful things that happened to you because of your father to shape you into a man who serves others without ever thinking about his own safety."

He blinked at her, all his air caught in his throat.

Was that really how she saw him?

But he could tell by the way she looked at him.

It was.

Chapter 13

"Check." Peyton gave a triumphant smile as she sat back in her seat.

"No way." Jared leaned forward to peer at the chess board, and Peyton couldn't stop herself from studying his face. The swelling in his eye had gone down, although the bruise was a sickly greenish blue. But that's not what drew her attention. Instead it was the relaxed set of his jaw, the new light in his eyes. He seemed to have become a different man since they'd talked in the park yesterday. A man more at peace with himself and the world around him. A man more willing to trust and open up.

It'd taken a lot of talking to convince him and the others that they should stay to finish out the trip. They'd only finally agreed to it when she promised she'd make sure she was with at least one of them at all times. So far today, Leah had popped in three times and Dan twice to offer to take a turn sitting around the fireplace with her so Jared could ski. But he refused to leave her side.

She couldn't deny the warmth that filled her with. Even if he was only doing it to keep Sawyer away. Fortunately, it seemed to be working. She hadn't seen Sawyer once all morning.

She and Jared had already played four games of chess, two games of Scrabble, and a single round of Pictionary that had them laughing so hard at her terrible drawings that they were gasping for breath. She couldn't deny that the morning had been nice. Comfortable.

Enough to make her want more.

But she pushed the thought aside. She was done trying to force things to happen. For now, it was enough to be talking to each other and having fun together again. She'd missed their friendship more than anything.

"Actually." Jared gave her a stunned smile. "That's checkmate. You beat me."

"I did?" Without thinking, she leaned over and hugged him. He'd taught her to play chess when they started dating, but she'd never beat him at it before.

"Wait a minute." She pulled back, trying to ignore the spicy sweet scent that lingered on her from the contact. "You let me win, didn't you?"

He raised his hands in front of him. "Nope. I promise. I know how much you hate that."

She grinned again. He'd tried to let her win a game of tennis once but had learned pretty quickly that wasn't going to score him any points with her.

Jared stretched his arms over his head, and she looked away so her eyes wouldn't be drawn to the way his t-shirt tightened against his biceps.

"You hungry?" Jared leaned forward to put the chess set away.

"Starved." On cue, her stomach rumbled, and Jared nudged her with a laugh. He'd always teased that he could set his clock by her stomach.

He stood and held out a hand to help her up. As soon as she was on her feet, he wrapped an arm around her back to help her hobble toward the dining room. The familiar feel of his arm around her was almost enough to make her forget that a whole year had gone by since he'd last held her close.

He steered her into the dining room, where a huge buffet had been set out. Peyton's mouth watered as the smell of lasagna wafted to her.

Jared led her to a table and pulled up an extra chair for her to prop her foot on. "I'll be right back with some food."

Her eyes followed him across the room. She wondered, did anyone else watching him see the demons that haunted him? Until yesterday, she'd had no idea. What he'd told her had broken her heart—both for the young boy who'd had to endure such treatment and for the man who carried around the weight of thinking he'd turn out like his father.

How could he believe that?

And how could he have let that keep them from having a life together?

But now that he'd told her, maybe he would rethink things.

She tried to tamp down the hope rising in her chest.

She'd promised she would wait on God's plans. And she had to accept that those plans most likely did not include Jared. They might not include anyone.

Then again, the way Jared was looking at her as he crossed the room carrying two plates stacked with food, maybe she wasn't so crazy to hope he was part of God's plan for her after all.

"They had those breadsticks you love." He passed her a plate as he sat, offering a smile that made her pulse do funny things. "I got you a few."

She glanced at the plate, and a laugh burst out of her. "I'll say." Breadsticks took up at least half of the space. Not that she was complaining.

She folded her hands and bowed her head to give silent thanks for the food.

Heavenly father, thank you—

"Do you mind if I pray with you?" Jared's voice was low, hesitant, but that didn't stop the enormous smile she felt stretching her lips. How had God answered that prayer before she'd even asked?

She reached across the table and gripped Jared's hands in hers. As they both bowed their heads, Jared began to pray. "Lord, we want to thank you for this meal you have provided. And that they had Peyton's favorite breadsticks."

She couldn't help the giggle that bubbled up. Who was this lighthearted man she was praying with?

"And thank you," Jared continued, "for keeping Peyton safe and for making her the strong, resilient, trusting woman she is. Please help her to seek after your plan for her life."

Peyton's smile melted, and she had to blink away the moisture that suddenly clung to her lashes. She'd always been touched when people prayed for her. But to hear

Jared praying for her? *That* arrowed right into her heart. In the best way.

"And—" Jared cleared his throat. "Thank you for using her and others to remind me that you are my perfect father."

"Amen," Peyton choked out. She had to keep her head bowed for a second after the prayer ended to get her heart under control.

"Thank you," she whispered as Jared slid his hands gently from hers.

His smile was soft and easy as he scooped a forkful of lasagna.

She started with a breadstick, savoring the garlic butter that coated the airy dough.

"How are things at the bakery?" Jared snatched one of her breadsticks, and she pretended to swat at him. He grinned and took a bite.

"It's going well. I'm getting to be pretty booked solid with weddings." The familiar pang shot through her at the mention of weddings, but it wasn't as sharp as usual. "I have one this weekend, actually. Since it's Valentine's Day, the cake is going to have a trail of fondant hearts all the way up the layers."

She broke off. Valentine's Day was the last thing they should be talking about together.

But he leaned forward, his warm gaze inviting her to continue.

"Anyway, if things keep up like this, I think I'm going to have to hire some help. At least for the summer."

"That's great. I'm proud of you."

She ducked her head and concentrated on cutting through a noodle. "Thanks."

She'd met Jared only days before she was scheduled to open her bakery in the cute little building that had drawn her to Hope Springs. He'd encouraged her when the idea of getting a single customer had been daunting. His support was a large part of what had given her the courage to keep going after her first wedding was a disaster, ending with the top of the cake on the floor.

"I wonder if—" But Jared broke off as the rest of their friends surrounded them. Was she only imagining the flash of disappointment in his eyes?

"Couldn't wait for us?" Ethan gave Jared's shoulder a light bump. Everyone's cheeks were pink, and they'd brought the fresh scent of the cold in with them.

"You know Peyton's stomach." Jared gave her a private smile that made her insides swoop the way they had when she and Jared first started dating.

Hopefully no one else noticed the blush she felt rising to her cheeks.

"You will not believe what happened to me out there." Leah plopped into the seat next to Peyton.

As she turned her attention to her friend, Peyton couldn't help sneaking a glance at Jared.

And if she wasn't mistaken, he was watching her, too.

Chapter 14

*J*ared couldn't stop smiling as he watched the staircase. He'd promised to sit with Peyton again today while the others skied, and he couldn't wait for her to get down here.

He'd insisted on being the one to stay with her yesterday only because he didn't trust Sawyer to stay away unless he knew Jared was with her. But as the day had gone on, he'd almost forgotten about Sawyer. He'd been so caught up in just being with Peyton again.

All those little things he'd fallen in love with—the things he'd spent the past year trying to forget—were still there. The way she tilted her head to the side when she laughed. The way she lifted a self-conscious hand to her hair whenever someone gazed at her for more than a few seconds. The way she could steal his breath with just a look.

And there were new things to fall in love with, too. Like the way she looked at him with complete trust even now that she knew the truth of his past. The way she smiled whenever he said her name. The way she'd rested her hands in his and let him pray for them.

By the time he'd said goodnight to her last night, he'd known he was a goner. He could tell himself he'd get over her someday. But it wasn't true. And he didn't really want it to be.

Because since yesterday, he'd been rethinking what he wanted for the future. And no matter what he did, he couldn't see that future without Peyton. But he didn't know how that could happen—*if* it could. Because the thought of marriage still terrified him. But if that was the only way he could be with her . . .

He forced his thoughts to a stop. For now, he'd just enjoy this day with her.

At last, he spotted her at the top of the steps with Leah and Emma. She wore a soft white sweater that made her hair and eyes look lighter than ever. Jared noted with satisfaction that she was limping less, though it meant he'd have fewer excuses to wrap his arm around her.

Her smile as she crossed the room toward him could have melted all the snow on the hills. If he had to guess, his probably matched.

"You sure you want to stay inside?" Leah got to him before Peyton did. "There's some pretty nice powder out there. I don't mind sitting with her."

"I'm staying." Jared practically growled at his friend, but she shot him a warning look.

"Jared, it's not—"

He held up a hand. "Don't say it's not fair."

"Well, it's not," Leah muttered as Peyton and Emma reached them.

"Good morning." His eyes locked on Peyton's, and he took a step closer.

"Morning."

But Leah stepped between them, turning to Peyton. "I was just telling Jared I'd sit with you so he could get some time on the slopes since it's our last day here."

"Oh, of course. You should ski." Her lips were still lifted in a smile, but it didn't mask the disappointment in her eyes.

If he hadn't already been decided, he was now. "I'm not skiing."

The light that returned to Peyton's eyes made the small sacrifice worth it.

"Fine." Leah huffed. "We'll be back at lunchtime. Maybe this time you two could wait for us before enjoying your romantic meal."

"We—"

But Peyton laid a gentle hand on his arm as Leah marched for the doors, Emma following with a helpless shrug. "She's just trying to protect me. Just like you are."

Jared nodded. He just wished he wasn't the one Leah was trying to protect Peyton from.

Not that he blamed her. He'd already broken her best friend's heart once. If he wasn't careful, he might do it again.

But he would be careful this time.

Starting with being sure of his own feelings before he talked to her about them.

Chapter 15

"Hey." The soft whisper was followed by the gentle press of lips to her hair, and Peyton snuggled closer.

She wasn't sure where she was, but she knew she was safe and warm, and that was enough. She never wanted to leave this spot.

"Hey." The whisper was more insistent this time, and a hand squeezed her shoulder.

"Mmm?"

"We should get you up to bed. You fell asleep."

She opened her eyes, letting them adjust to the low lights, the dark lobby fireplace. An arm was wrapped protectively around her, and her face was pressed into something solid yet comfortable. She jerked upright as she realized it was Jared's shoulder.

"Sorry, I—"

But he smiled at her. "You were in the middle of telling me about the wedding with the flamingos, and you fell asleep."

"I did?" She rubbed at her eyes, trying to work out the tangles in her thoughts. "Sorry if I was boring you with my stories."

"You never bore me." He brushed a piece of hair off her cheek. The move was gentle and familiar, and she couldn't help leaning into his hand.

"Jared?"

"Yeah?"

She meant to tell him she was sorry she'd crossed the line and fallen asleep on his shoulder, but instead, she leaned closer and pressed her lips to his.

He stiffened and inhaled sharply, but then his arms came around her, and his lips responded softly, gently. This was not at all the hungry kiss Sawyer had tried to force on her. Jared's kiss made her feel cherished and protected.

Loved.

Slowly, she pulled back.

The past two days with Jared had been nothing short of perfect. But it was late, and tomorrow they'd go back to their lives in Hope Springs. And she'd have to face the fact that as much as she wanted a future with him, that didn't seem to be God's plan. Or Jared's.

"I'm sorry." The whisper barely made it past her lips. "I shouldn't have—"

A gentle finger tipped her chin up until she was gazing into Jared's eyes. What she saw there made everything in her warm.

"It's okay." One side of Jared's mouth lifted, but his eyes remained totally serious. "Peyton, I've tried to move on. Tried to pretend I don't still feel something for you. But the truth is—" He slid his hands into hers. "I still love you."

He didn't move after he said it. Just waited, watching her. She wondered vaguely if he was even breathing, he was so still.

Then again, she wasn't absolutely sure she was breathing, either.

"I love you, too." She closed her eyes. These next words were going to be the hardest she'd ever had to say in her life. "But we want different things for the future. And I don't think—"

"No, wait, Peyton." He slid closer, gripping both of her hands in his and bringing them to his lips. The kiss he pressed to them was so tender it made her heart squeeze.

"I've been thinking about that. And I can't lose you again. I won't. And if that means I need to marry you, then—" He blew out a quick breath, it's warmth tickling her fingers. "Maybe I could consider marriage. Someday."

Her eyes filled. If he'd said those words to her a year ago, she would have been in a dress shop by morning. But she wasn't going to try to force her future anymore.

"I can't do this again, Jared." The whisper scraped against her vocal cords. "I tried so hard for so long to make God give me a future with you. But I'm giving over the reins to him now."

Jared's shoulders sagged, and he directed his gaze to the empty fireplace. "Is this because—" He drew a labored breath. "Is this because of what I told you the other day?"

"No." She grabbed his arm and waited for him to look at her. "It has nothing to do with that. I'm so grateful you told me. And if anything, it makes me love you more. To know what you grew up with and to see the man you became in spite of it. But I don't want you to marry me just because you think it's the only way to hold onto me. If I do get married, I want it to be to someone who wants to build a life with me. Who's committed to forever together."

"I do want—" He lifted her hands to his heart, but she gently pulled them back.

"I'm sorry, Jared."

He looked away and swallowed hard. When he turned back, his red eyes almost made her take back everything she'd said.

But she had to give this over to God.

Had to trust that he had the best plan for her future.

Jared nodded slowly, pressing his lips together. Then he stood. "Let's get you up to bed."

She pushed to her feet. Her body felt heavier than it had ever been as she followed him.

Upstairs, he stepped into his room without another word. She watched his door close, then leaned on her own and let the silent tears come.

She knew trusting God with her future was the right thing to do.

So why did it feel like she was cutting out her own heart all over again?

Chapter 16

Jared rattled the doors of Hope Church one more time, as if expecting them to magically unlock for him. He didn't know why he'd thought the doors would be open on a Saturday afternoon, anyway. He only knew that he needed to talk to someone, and Dan had offered, but he didn't know how else to get ahold of him.

The drive home from Tamarack Wednesday morning had been torture. Every time he looked into the rearview mirror, he'd caught a glimpse of Peyton's puffy eyes and raw cheeks.

He didn't imagine he looked much better after a sleepless night spent trying to figure out how he'd ever let her go in the first place.

He'd thought being home in Hope Springs would soothe the piercing pain that jolted through him with every heartbeat. But he'd been wrong.

Instead, his thoughts had locked on her.

Peyton had said she needed a man who wanted to build a future with her. Who was committed to her forever. Didn't that describe him exactly?

Except for one thing. He couldn't promise her marriage. Not yet. Maybe not ever.

Still, the thought of marrying her had hovered in his thoughts over the past few days like a tantalizing mirage. One he didn't dare approach. He'd spent all of his life so sure that he was never intended for marriage. That the only way to make sure he didn't turn into his father was to remain alone.

Finally, last night he had dropped to his knees next to his bed. He'd prayed for God to make him content with letting go of Peyton so she could have the future she deserved.

Instead, the longer he prayed, the more at peace he'd felt with the thought of marrying her.

But how did he know that wasn't only his own selfish desire instead of what was best for Peyton?

Because as much as he would give everything to be with her, he wanted even more for her to have the future she prayed for—the future God had planned for her.

He'd been hoping Dan could shed some light on the whole knotted mess, but apparently he was going to have to figure this out on his own and pray he didn't do anything to hurt Peyton's chances for happiness.

He was about to get into his car when someone called his name.

He swiveled in search of the voice.

"Over here."

Jared looked over his shoulder and spotted Dan in the snowy yard of the big brick house next to the church. Dan lifted a hand and jogged over.

"I got a call from Mrs. Reinhold on the other side of the church. She was all worked up that someone was trying to break into the building." He laughed and clapped Jared on the shoulder. "I assume that was you?"

Jared joined in the laughter. Much as he hadn't wanted to like Dan, he had to admit the guy was easy to get along with.

"Guilty as charged."

"That's a relief. So what were you after?"

Jared focused on the asphalt parking lot, stained gray from the layers of salt that had been spread on it during the last snowstorm. "I was looking for you, actually."

If Dan was surprised, he hid it well. "Great. You found me. What's up?"

Jared kicked at an ice chunk that had been left behind by the snowplow. "I was wondering if your offer to talk was still good."

"Of course. Come on in."

Jared followed Dan as he led the way across the lawn and into the front door of the old house.

"Don't mind the boxes. Still getting unpacked." Dan wove through the maze of boxes to a worn couch at the far side of the living room. "Have a seat. I'd offer you something to drink, but all I have is water, and I haven't found the glasses yet."

"That's okay." Jared sat, his leg bouncing against the couch cushion. Now that he was here, he had no idea how to ask the question that had been eating at him all night. So he blurted it out. "How do I know God's plan?"

If Dan found the question abrupt, he didn't let on. "His plan for what?"

"Me, I guess." Jared raised his hands helplessly. He didn't know what he was looking for exactly, so how could he expect Dan to provide it? "I mean, that pastor at Tamarack said God has a plan for each of us, right? But how do we know what that plan is?"

Dan studied him, but Jared didn't feel uncomfortable under the younger man's scrutiny. "Remember the verse the pastor quoted? Jeremiah 29:11? It says that God has plans to prosper us and not to harm us." He lifted his hands in front of him. "That's it. That's God's plan for us."

"But—" Jared spluttered. "That's not a plan. I need something more specific. More detailed. Like a sign, I guess. Or something. Anything." Desperation made his voice go up, but he didn't care. There had to be more.

Dan gave a gentle laugh, but Jared could tell it wasn't at his expense. "You have no idea how many times I've wanted that, too. But the thing is, God's plan is for us to honor and serve him. And there are a lot of ways we can do that—many of them not necessarily better or worse than others." He twirled his thumbs around each other, not looking at Jared. "Do you mind if I ask you something?"

Jared grimaced and braced for Dan's interrogation. For his reprimand that if Jared only prayed harder or went to church more or was a better Christian, he'd know God's will without having to ask such stupid questions.

"Is this about Peyton?" Dan met his eyes as he asked.

Jared startled. How had Dan known?

But he nodded. There was no point in denying it.

"I don't know your story, aside from what Leah told me," Dan said.

"She—"

Dan held up a hand. "All she said was that you two used to date but that you wouldn't marry her, so you broke up."

Dan's eyes drilled into his, but there wasn't any judgment there, and Jared's chest loosened.

"And now you're wondering if you made the right decision."

Well, the guy was good. Jared had to give him that much. "Okay, pastor or mind reader?"

"Definitely pastor. Doesn't take a mind reader to see how you feel about her."

Jared nodded slowly. "But is how I feel about her enough? How do I know God's plan for us? How do I know I'm even fit to be a husband?"

Dan was silent for a moment, seeming to weigh his response, and Jared's heart sank. He'd known it was too much to expect that it would be God's will for him to marry Peyton.

"God's plan is for you to honor and serve him, whether you marry or not," Dan finally said. "And if you do marry, his plan is for you to honor and serve your wife. To build her up in her faith. To be there for her, to protect her, to love her through everything. So I guess the real question is, do you love her?"

"You just said you know I do."

"I know, but I want to hear from you how you feel about her."

"I feel—" Jared cleared his throat. How did he put the depth of his feelings for Peyton into words? "She's the best part of me. She makes me want to be this fantastic man she seems to think I am. This past year, I've felt like I was missing a part of me. Not an arm or a leg, but something inside me that I can't name. Something vital. Something I can't live without."

Dan's eyes gleamed as he stared at him. "I think you just answered your own question."

"I did?"

But he knew it, too.

And he knew what he had to do.

Chapter 17

*P*eyton hummed as she placed the fondant hearts on the cake she'd just finished stacking. It was one of the most breathtaking cakes she'd ever made, if she did say so herself.

"Aren't you cheerful." Leah snatched an extra fondant heart and took a big bite. "Oh . . . This is so good. What's in it?"

"Vanilla bean paste." Peyton grabbed one of the extra hearts and sneaked her own nibble. The creamy vanilla rolled over her tongue.

"So what's up with the humming?" Leah shoved the rest of the heart into her mouth.

Peyton shrugged. "Just happy, I guess."

She shouldn't be, really. Every time she thought of Jared, she still felt a lingering ache. But she was content with her decision to wait on the Lord's plan. She trusted that one way or another, he'd lead her to it—whatever it might be. She only hoped she'd recognize it when he did.

"There." She placed the last heart. "You want to help me get this to the cake table?" She checked the time. She was cutting this one closer to the start of the reception than she liked, but she'd wanted to get everything perfect for this couple's Valentine's Day wedding.

"I'm happy for you." Leah held the kitchen door open so Peyton could push the cart with the cake through.

Fortunately, the swelling in her foot had gone down almost completely, and she could walk without limping at all.

"Thanks. I am, too." Peyton couldn't help smiling as she gazed around the elegant ballroom. Thin copper hearts wrapped with white lights hung from the ceiling, and delicate red glass tea lights decorated each table. The whole room said *love*.

Instead of the usual pang of jealousy, Peyton felt only a faint wistfulness. Maybe she'd have her own wedding like this someday. But until then, she'd be content with this moment in her life.

She wheeled the cart to the round table that had been set aside, waiting for Leah to take a position on the other end of the tray so they could transfer the six-layer cake. She took a deep breath. This was always the most nerve-wracking part of any wedding. One wobble and all her hard work would be destroyed—not to mention a wedding ruined.

But they managed to transfer the cake without incident. After a few touch-ups with her scraper, Peyton was satisfied with her masterpiece.

She gave Leah a quick hug. "I'll get out of your hair now so you can finish up with the dinner prep."

Her friend studied her. "What are you doing tonight? You want me to come over when I'm done here? We can have an anti-Valentine's Day or something."

But before Peyton could answer, Leah's phone rang. She pulled it out of her pocket and rolled her eyes. "Hold that thought."

Peyton wandered among the tables as she waited for Leah to get off the phone.

She couldn't help smiling as she hummed another verse of her favorite Christian song. She appreciated Leah's offer to keep her distracted tonight. But she didn't need an anti-Valentine's Day party.

A year ago, she'd been sure she'd never be happy again. But surrendering herself to God's will had filled her with a kind of joy she'd never known before.

Not that it was easy or that it meant it didn't hurt to let go of her own dreams.

But it took away the constant pressure of trying to make things happen in her own time. The constant despair when things didn't work out according to her plans.

Leah bustled up behind her. "That was one of my waiters. Who was supposed to be here an hour ago. Calling to say he quit." Leah hesitated. "I hate to ask—"

But Peyton was already rolling up her sleeves. "Where do you need me?"

Peyton stacked her tray with the last plates of cake. Her ankle had started to pulse from rushing around the reception hall all night delivering food and coffee and cake, but it had actually been kind of fun. Usually she was gone long before the cake was served, so she never got to see people's reactions as they ate it. Plenty of people had told her after the fact how much they loved it, of course. But watching them actually savor it brought a whole new level of satisfaction.

She lifted the tray to her shoulder. Miraculously, she'd made it through the night without dropping anything. Maybe some of her mother's grace was finally manifesting in her.

131

As she started across the ballroom toward the farthest table, she let herself observe the bride and groom at the front of the room. The groom was leaning toward his new wife, a huge smile lighting his face. After a second, she smiled, too, then burst into laughter.

Peyton felt her own lips ease into a grin. She only knew the couple from the meetings they'd had to discuss their cake order, but they seemed sweet. She was glad everything had gone so perfectly for their special day.

"Peyton!" The shout from behind her sounded strangely like Jared.

She jumped and whirled toward it. The quick movement made the tray teeter on her arm. She threw up her other hand to steady it.

But it was too late.

One of the plates slid off. Peyton watched, helpless, as it hit the floor with a crash.

She closed her eyes as every head in the room swiveled toward her.

This was not happening.

She had not just ruined this sweet couple's wedding day.

When she opened her eyes, they landed on Jared, who was barreling across the room, weaving between chairs as he made his way toward her. His face was set into an expression she didn't recognize.

But she didn't have time for this right now. She had to get this mess cleaned up.

"I'm sorry," she mumbled to no one in particular as she stepped around the splattered cake and broken china. She needed a broom or a mop or something. Plus, she still had to deliver the rest of the cake slices on her tray.

But Jared had shoved his way between the tables and blocked her path.

"Peyton, wait."

"I have to clean this up, Jared." She tried to keep her voice low so they wouldn't create any more of a disturbance. "What are you even doing here?" As far as she knew, he didn't know the bride and groom. And he wasn't exactly dressed for a wedding in his jeans and polo shirt.

"I went to your house, but you weren't there, and I remembered you had a wedding, so I called around and . . ." He gestured to the room, his eyes widening as if he'd just noticed they had an audience. "I need to talk to you."

She tried to get past him, but there wasn't enough room to step around him without smacking a guest in the head with her cake tray.

"Jared, whatever it is, it's going to have to wait."

"This has waited too long, Peyton. It can't wait any longer." He took the tray from her and gave it to a guest at the nearest table.

"What are you—" But before she could comprehend what he was doing, he'd grabbed her hands and dropped to one knee in front of her.

"Jared, what's going on?" But then it dawned on her.

Her bottom lip started to tremble. There was no way he was really going to do this.

But he reached into his pocket and withdrew a white gold ring with a marquis cut diamond. The exact ring she'd looked at a thousand times in the jewelry store but had never mentioned to him.

She was suddenly aware of the silence that had fallen in the room. A quick glance showed that everyone had turned toward them. She tried to tug her hand back. She was supposed to be working right now.

But Jared squeezed her hand and slid closer. "Peyton, I didn't think I'd ever ask any woman this question. I thought my past meant I was destined to live my life alone. But you showed me what love is. You showed me who I really am."

Somewhere in the back of her mind, Peyton was aware of all the eyes on them. But she couldn't have walked away now if the building had been on fire. She had to know what he was going to say next.

"I've been searching and searching for some grand plan. For some sign. But it turns out it was right in front of me all along. Because God's plan is for me to honor and serve my wife."

She closed her eyes. She'd never thought she'd hear that word from his mouth.

When she opened them again, his eyes were shimmering.

He lifted her hand to his lips and dropped the lightest kiss there. "Peyton, will you let me honor and serve and love you all my days? Will you be my wife?"

Peyton pressed her lips tight to hold back the flood of emotion. These were the words she'd prayed so long and so hard to hear.

But Jared had been set against marriage his entire life. He might think he was ready to commit to it, but how could she know for certain?

Which was why she had to give him an answer that ripped at her own heart.

"I don't know."

Chapter 18

The whole room seemed to spin, and Jared felt as if he'd floated up out of his body and was looking down on this wedding where some fool was pouring his heart out in front of a room full of strangers who were shifting uncomfortably in their seats.

"You don't know?" he managed to croak. How could this be happening? The one thing he'd been certain of was that Peyton wanted to marry. Now he was offering that, and she was saying no?

Peyton pulled her hand back from his, and this time he let her.

"I'm sorry, Jared," she whispered, then spun toward the kitchen.

He dropped his chin to his chest. He'd been so sure of this.

Was still so sure.

So why was he just sitting here?

He pushed to his feet and ran after her. He was not going to lose her this time.

Just as she was about to push the kitchen door open, he overtook her.

"Peyton."

"Just go, Jared." The tears on her cheeks almost broke him. He could see it in her eyes. She wanted to say yes, but she was afraid.

"Please, Peyton. You have to understand something. The idea of marrying terrifies me."

She closed her eyes, and he rushed on before she could shut him out. "But you want to know what terrifies me more?"

He waited for her to open her eyes again. To look into his. "The thought of not marrying you, of not spending my life as your husband—that terrifies me more than anything. Because I belong to you—heart, body, soul. I've prayed about this, Peyton. I've prayed for your future and for mine. For our future."

Her tears fell faster, and he moved closer, grasping her hands in his. "What is it?" he whispered, these words meant only for her.

"What if you change your mind?"

He lifted a hand to wipe at her tears, giving her a gentle smile. Didn't she see? She had his heart. "The thing that scared me about marriage was making a promise I couldn't keep. A promise to love you and protect you forever. But now I know that I couldn't stop doing those things—ever. And I'm promising you, right here and right now—" He glanced over his shoulder to see that all eyes were still on them, then turned back to her, raising his voice so that everyone in the room would hear. "With all these people as my witnesses, I promise you that I will marry you one year from today. On your favorite day of the year." He swallowed. "If you'll have me."

The smile spread across her lips so slowly, he wasn't sure if it was there at all at first.

But then she laughed, a light laugh full of hope and joy. "Yes, Jared, I'll marry you."

"You will?" He couldn't move at first. He was sure he'd heard wrong. But she was still laughing and crying, and she held out her hand for the ring he still gripped in his.

He stared at her hand, suddenly awestruck that this woman would have him. "Are you sure?"

Behind them, a few people chuckled.

"I'm positive."

He was sure everyone must be able to see the outline of his heart under his shirt because there was no way his chest could contain such joy.

He slid the ring onto her finger. She looked at it for a second, then sprang forward and threw her arms around him.

He wrapped his arms around her and leaned to whisper in her ear. "I love you."

She nodded against him. "I love you, too."

Behind them, the wedding guests burst into applause.

"Congratulations," someone said into the microphone. Jared assumed it was the groom, but he didn't look.

He couldn't take his eyes off his future bride.

He lowered his head and brought his lips to hers. The smile on her face when he pulled back strengthened something inside him.

He would work every day for the rest of his life to keep that smile there.

Starting with today.

"I think I have a new favorite holiday." He laced his fingers in hers.

"Oh, yeah?" She tugged him into the kitchen and spun in his arms, tilting her face up toward his. "And what holiday would that be?" She was close enough that her breath skated lightly across his lips.

He grinned and kissed her again. "Every day with you."

Thank you for reading NOT UNTIL THIS MOMENT! I hope you loved Jared and Peyton's story! Catch up with them as their friend Violet finds love in NOT UNTIL YOU, another emotional, uplifting story set in Hope Springs!

And be sure to sign up for my newsletter to get Ethan and Ariana's story, NOT UNTIL CHRISTMAS, as a free gift. Sign up at www.valeriembodden.com/gift!

A preview of Not Until You

Nate squinted into the blinding expanse of the parking lot. Had the world always been this bright, or did it only seem that way after seeing it through bars and walls for the past seven years?

His gaze roved the cars scattered throughout the lot. He'd written home to let his parents know today was his release date, but they'd never written back. Not that he'd expected a reply. After seven years without contact, a person kind of gave up.

Still, he'd half hoped, half dreaded that at least one of them would be here to meet him. He had a grand total of ten dollars to his name. Which left him with the options of sleeping on a park bench tonight or hitchhiking the fifty miles back to his hometown.

"Nathan." There was no mistaking his father's stern voice.

Nate turned to find his dad standing several rows away. He probably couldn't bring himself to come any closer to the building that proved his son was the worst kind of screw up. Dad looked older than the last time Nate had seen him, his once salt and pepper hair now all salt, his suit fitting him more loosely than it used to. He stood as stoic and unsmiling as ever, though.

Nate forced himself to breathe as he approached his father. Forced himself to keep his shoulders straight and his chin up, the way Dad had drilled into him.

Two feet in front of Dad, he stopped and held out his right hand. Dad looked at it a moment, then slapped a piece of paper into it.

Nate flipped it over. A slow churn started in his gut.

"A bus ticket?" He swallowed the bile rising at the back of his throat. The only thing that had gotten him through the past seven years was the promise of going home. Of making things right. Of making up for what he'd done.

He'd work the rest of his life to do it if that's what it took.

"Get in the car. Your bus leaves in twenty minutes." Dad disappeared into the driver's door without another glance at Nate.

Nate stood frozen a moment, then moved toward the passenger door. What had he expected? That Dad would welcome him home with open arms like some sort of long-lost son?

The moment Nate closed his door, Dad backed out of the parking spot.

"Can't I at least see Mom first?" He pressed his lips together, trying to push down the emotion building in his chest. "And Kayla?"

"The bus will take you to Hope Springs."

"Where?" Nate had never heard of the place. "Why?"

But before Dad even threw him the dark look, Nate knew. He was being banished.

"We just bought out a property management firm there." Dad's voice, the voice Nate had remembered for its resonance, was flatter than the cornfields that stretched in every direction around them. "It's in pretty bad shape. You're going to make it profitable. I expect weekly progress reports."

"Dad, I don't want—"

"Card's in the suitcase." Dad plowed on as if Nate hadn't spoken. "There's a law office next door. They have the key. At least one of our buildings has an empty apartment. You can live there."

"Dad—"

"There's a bag in the back."

Nate swiveled to look over his shoulder. A small suitcase rested on the backseat, as if Nate were going on some sort of vacation.

"There are clothes in it. Some money." Dad's head didn't move so much as a centimeter.

"I don't want money. I want—"

"Frankly, Nathan, I don't care what you want. This is what you get. You made your choices. Now you have to deal with the consequences."

Nate stared at Dad. Didn't he think Nate knew that? That he'd spend the rest of his life living with the consequences of his actions?

He wanted to argue. To plead. But he'd learned early on that once Dad's mind was made up, nothing was going to change it.

A sharp silence sliced the air between them. It took Nate two tries before he could open his mouth to tell Dad what he'd needed to say for seven years. "Dad, I know it's not enough, but I want to say I'm sorry. I don't expect you to forgive me. But you have to know, if I could trade places with Kayla, I would. I—"

145

"But you can't. And all the sorries in the world aren't going to change that." Still that flat voice. Anger would be better. Or sadness. Anything but this stony, emotionless man.

"I know they're not." Nate said it so quietly he wasn't sure Dad heard him. He made himself speak up. "Can you at least tell me how Kayla is?" Seven years with no word on his sister's condition had been the worst part of his punishment.

Dad's jaw tightened. "You ruined her life, Nathan. And mine. Your mother's. You expect me to sit here and chat with you like we're old buddies?"

"No, but—"

"You know, Nathan, when I think about how excited we were when we learned your mother was expecting you— We thought you would be such a blessing." He let out a sharp, humorless laugh. "Some blessing. We'd have been better off if you'd never been born."

Nate turned toward the window and scrunched his eyes shut, pinching the bridge of his nose between his fingers.

He deserved every one of those hateful words. He'd told himself the same thing every day for the past seven years. But hearing them from his dad's mouth—the same man who had read him bedtime stories and played airplane with him and told him he loved him—sliced through every vital organ in his body.

Dad pulled up to the curb outside the bus station. Nate mashed his teeth together and grabbed the door handle. "Please, Dad. Just let me say goodbye to Mom and Kayla."

Dad stared straight out the windshield. "Show me you're not the worst mistake of my life, and maybe someday you can see them again. Until then, I'm not letting you near my family."

Nate wanted to say they were his family, too. That he would do anything for them. But his words would never convince his father. He'd have to make a success of this new job Dad had assigned him. No matter how much he hated it.

If it meant he could see his mother and sister again, it would be worth it.

More Hope Springs Books

While the books in the Hope Springs series are linked, each is a complete romance featuring a different couple and can be read in any order. Wondering whose story is whose? Here's a helpful list:

Not Until Christmas (Ethan & Ariana)

Not Until Forever (Sophie & Spencer)

Not Until This Moment (Jared & Peyton)

Not Until You (Nate & Violet)

Not Until Us (Dan & Jade)

Not Until Christmas Morning (Leah & Austin)

Not Until This Day (Tyler & Isabel)

Not Until Someday (Grace & Levi)

Not Until Now (Cam & Kayla)

Not Until Then (Bethany & James)

Not Until The End (Emma & Owen)

And Don't Miss the
River Falls Series

Set in the small town of River Falls, nestled in the Smoky Mountains of Tennessee.

Pieces of Forever (Joseph & Ava)
Songs of Home (Lydia & Liam)
Memories of the Heart (Simeon & Abigail)
Whispers of Truth (Benjamin & Summer)

Want to know when my next book releases?

You can follow me on Amazon to be the first to know when my next book releases! Just visit amazon.com/author/valeriembodden and click the follow button.

Acknowledgements

What a blessing that I never run out of people to thank in the acknowledgements section of my books. First, of course, thank you to my perfect heavenly Father, the source of all love. As his Word tells us, "We love because he first loved us" (1 John 4:19).

And speaking of love, I thank the love of my life, my husband Josh, for his continued support and love. If it weren't for him, I might still be dreaming about writing and publishing novels instead of taking the leap into doing it.

Thank you also to my children, who still love our annual Valentine's Day tea parties and who let me hug them in public (sometimes, at least).

And to my parents, my sister, my in-laws, and my extended family: your love, support, and encouragement have lifted me up as I've embarked on this adventure, and I am grateful for each one of you.

A special thank you goes out to my advance readers, who didn't blink at the tight timeline I told them I was hoping to follow for this book—and who read it even faster than I asked and then told me it was their favorite yet! So thank you to Jen Ellenson, Rachel Kozinski, Josie Bartelt, and Connie Gronholz. You are amazing ladies, and I'm so thankful to have each of you in my life.

My acknowledgements wouldn't be complete if I didn't say thank you to you as well, my wonderful reader friends! Thanks for coming along with me on this journey. I pray that you may be blessed through this book and encouraged in your walk of faith.

God's richest blessings to you!

About the Author

Valerie M. Bodden has three great loves: Jesus, her family, and books. And chocolate (okay, four great loves). She is living out her happily ever after with her high-school-sweetheart-turned-husband and their four children. Her life wouldn't make a terribly exciting book, as it has a happy beginning and middle, and someday when she goes to her heavenly home, it will have a happy end.

She was born and raised in Wisconsin but recently moved with her family to Texas, where they're all getting used to the heat (she doesn't miss the snow even a little bit, though the rest of the family does) and saying y'all instead of you guys.

Valerie writes emotion-filled Christian fiction that weaves real-life problems, real-life people, and real-life faith. Her characters may (okay, will) experience some heartache along the way, but she will always give them a happy ending.

Feel free to stop by www.valeriembodden.com to say hi. She loves visitors! And while you're there, you can sign up for your free story.

Printed in Great Britain
by Amazon